Celebrations
at Thrush Green

* * *

Miss Read

Illustrated by J. S. Goodall

An Orion paperback

First published in Great Britain in 1992
by Michael Joseph Ltd
This paperback edition published in 2009
by Orion Books
an imprint of The Orion Publishing Group Ltd,
Orion House, 5 Upper St Martin's Lane,
London WC2H 9EA

An Hachette UK company

3 5 7 9 10 8 6 4

A CIP catalogue record for this book is
available from the British Library.

ISBN 978-0-7528-8426-4

Typeset at the Spartan Press Ltd,
Lymington, Hants

Printed and bound in Great Britain by
Clays Ltd, St Ives plc

The Orion Publishing Group's policy is to use papers that
are natural, renewable and recyclable products and
made from wood grown in sustainable forests. The logging
and manufacturing processes are expected to conform to
the environmental regulations of the country of origin.

www.orionbooks.co.uk

Miss Read, or in real life Dora Saint, was a teacher by profession who started writing after the Second World War, beginning with light essays written for *Punch* and other journals. She then wrote on educational and country matters and worked as a scriptwriter for the BBC. Miss Read was married to a schoolmaster for sixty-four years until his death in 2004, and they had one daughter.

Miss Read was awarded an MBE in the 1998 New Year Honours list for her services to literature. She was the author of many immensely popular books, including two autobiographical works, but it was her novels of English rural life for which she was best known. The first of these, *Village School*, was published in 1955, and Miss Read continued to write about the fictional villages of Fairacre and Thrush Green for many years. She lived near Newbury in Berkshire until her death in 2012.

To Babs
with love

CONTENTS

* * *

CONTENTS

1. ONE WET DAY

One wet November morning, Winnie Bailey stood at her bedroom window and surveyed the rain-drenched view of Thrush Green.

Usually at this time of the morning, a little past nine o'clock, things were stirring. One or two late arrivals at the school across the green would be running in breathlessly. Percy Hodge's milk float would be making its slow way from house to house. A few housewives would be hurrying downhill to the shops in Lulling, baskets in hand.

But today there was little movement. A wet umbrella passed below, its carrier hidden from Winnie's view. A duster flapped from an upstairs window of The Two Pheasants across the green, hard by the school, and two excited dogs cavorted by the deserted and dripping children's play area.

Winnie Bailey had lived at Thrush Green for over fifty years, ever since she arrived as the bride of young Dr Bailey. He had died some years before, but Winnie stayed on in the house she loved, sharing it with Jenny, her friend and companion.

She could hear Jenny now, singing some unrecognizable tune as she washed up the breakfast things. And here she was, Winnie told herself briskly, supposed to be dusting bedrooms, and instead she was idling her time away gazing at the rain!

She was about to turn to her duties when she saw a small black car moving decorously along the road opposite, skirting

The Two Pheasants and the school and finally drawing up outside Harold Shoosmith's house. Surely it was the rector's car, thought Winnie, peering again through the rain-spotted window, dusting forgotten.

A small chubby man emerged from the driver's seat and hurried through the downpour to the shelter of the Shoo-smiths' porch. The Reverend Charles Henstock, rector of Thrush Green and vicar of Lulling, was paying an early morning call on his old friend.

Winnie took up her duster again, and speculated.

'Come in! Come in!' cried Harold. 'Good grief, man, haven't you got a raincoat?'

'I didn't think I'd need it,' replied Charles.

'Let's have your jacket,' said his host, stripping it from the rector's back and shaking it energetically. 'Isobel's away for two nights, in Sussex. Come into the kitchen, it's warmer.'

The two men settled at the kitchen table. Outside, the rain lashed at the window, and gurgled in the gutter. A pigeon sat hunched on the bird-table, presumably seeking shelter rather than food, raindrops dripping from the little roof above it.

'Coffee?' asked Harold.

The rector shook his head. He had turned round to try to extricate an envelope from the inside pocket of his wet jacket.

'Such a strange letter,' he said, puffing slightly as he pulled it free. 'It arrived yesterday but I didn't have a chance to get in touch with you.'

He handed it to Harold and sat back to watch his friend's reaction as he read.

Harold skipped the preliminaries and perused the second paragraph onward with growing concentration. He read:

I have been clearing up my late aunt's effects recently, and came across some letters and a diary among her papers. The letters are from one Nathaniel Patten and are addressed to the Reverend Octavius Fennel of Thrush Green. The diary, which also appears to be an account book, is that of Mr Fennel.

I have no idea how these papers came into my aunt's possession, but she lived for a time near Thrush Green, and only moved here to the Lake District a few years ago to be near her family, as she was becoming infirm.

It seems right to me that these papers should be returned to the church, and I shall be pleased to let you have them if you send word.

Harold peered closely at the signature. 'Can't make out the chap's name. "Wellbeloved"? "Wobblefoot"?'

'Wilberforce,' said the rector. 'And isn't it extraordinary?'

'It is indeed,' agreed Harold warmly. 'We must get hold of these letters. To think that we shall see Nathaniel's actual handwriting after all this time.'

The rector smiled indulgently upon his friend. He knew how much Nathaniel Patten meant to him.

Nathaniel had been a Thrush Green boy born and bred in Queen Victoria's reign, and had travelled to Africa as a missionary. There Nathaniel had set up a church, a mission hall, a school and the beginnings of a medical centre. His project flourished, and Nathaniel Patten was greatly loved by the people he cared for.

His reputation grew over the years. His devotion, wisdom and sound common sense were widely recognized for miles around his settlement, but those in Thrush Green had forgotten the young man who had left his home.

He never in his lifetime returned. His duties and shortage of funds kept him at his post. But at his death his body was returned, at the express wish and expense of the Reverend Octavius Fennel, who himself conducted the funeral service.

Elderly inhabitants of Thrush Green and Lulling had memories of their parents' respect for the former rector. The Reverend Octavius Fennel had befriended the young Nathaniel, encouraging him in his missionary work and helping, it was believed, with financial support.

It was known that Octavius dearly wished Nathaniel to take Holy Orders, but the strongly evangelical nature of the younger man would not allow him to accept all the tenets of the established Church of England, and he was never ordained.

Over the years, Nathaniel was forgotten by Thrush Green. It was not until Harold Shoosmith had arrived some years before that Thrush Green folk became aware that it was the birthplace of their most distinguished son.

In a strange way, it was Nathaniel Patten who had brought Harold Shoosmith to Thrush Green. Harold had lived near the community in Africa where the Victorian missionary had worked, bringing spiritual comfort and practical help to hundreds of his flock. By the time Harold was there, Nathaniel was dead, but his work still thrived and the small stone cross which was his memorial was kept immaculate with lime-wash, and flowers always lay at its foot.

The tales of the villagers about their hero moved Harold deeply, and when he had decided to retire he was excited to find that a house in Nathaniel's birthplace was on the market. It suited him well, and he had become one of Thrush Green's most active and well-liked residents.

It was something of a shock to him to realize that Nathaniel meant nothing to his neighbours. His tombstone was overgrown, the inscription indecipherable. No one, it seemed, had heard of him. The parish register noted his birth and burial, and that seemed to be the only mention of the great man.

Harold set about remedying this matter, and was instrumental in getting a statue put up on the green on the occasion of the hundredth anniversary of Nathaniel's birth. It now stood, a matter of pride and affection, and Nathaniel had been restored to the hearts of those in Thrush Green.

Harold and Charles had worked hard to trace any descendants of Nathaniel when the business of the memorial statue was afoot. Evidently he had married whilst abroad. His wife, debilitated by the rigours of the climate, had died giving birth to a daughter.

When the child was old enough, she had been sent to friends in Yorkshire to be housed and educated. She had married a man called Michael Mulloy, borne a son and daughter, and the family had moved to Pembrokeshire to work on a farm.

Times were hard in the 1930s, and the Mulloys lived in poverty. The son, William, grew up to be a wild youth. The daughter, Mary, never married.

William married in the 1950s and his wife soon discovered that she had made a serious mistake. He was a drunkard, and violent when in his cups. She lived in daily fear of his attacks upon her and upon their young daughter Dulcie, named after Nathaniel's daughter.

Fortunately, his sister Mary, who lived near by, was a strong character who had no time for William, but gave support to his wife and child. It was she who had kept Nathaniel's letters to her mother, and who told Dulcie of the wonderful work he had done. Mary had died when Dulcie was a grown woman.

Harold and Charles had met William briefly in Wales where he farmed a few acres. He was a dissolute uncouth fellow who had no time for Nathaniel's memory. At the time of their meeting he had left his wife and daughter, Dulcie, and was living with a woman near by.

What had happened to William Mulloy, his poor wife and little Dulcie? the kind-hearted rector often wondered. Harold, of sterner stuff, did not waste his energies in thinking about them.

Harold continued to hold the letter, his face alight with enthusiasm. 'I can't believe it!'

'I thought I would reply to Mr Wilberforce today,' said Charles, 'and say how glad we would be to have these papers, and perhaps he would be kind enough to post them to us.'

'*Post!*' cried Harold. 'Dear old Nathaniel's letters? I wouldn't trust those to the *post*!'

'Oh, come!' responded the rector. 'Do be fair. How often does the post go astray?'

'When the post *does* go astray,' replied his friend forcefully, 'I don't know about it, do I? No, I'm not risking this lot to the post. If it comes to that I'll go up myself and fetch them.'

'Then what do you suggest I write?'

'Don't write. Telephone. Let's do it now.'

'But it's scarcely nine thirty! He'll be at work.'

'Then we'll ring him at work.'

Charles felt helpless in the face of such ruthlessness. He watched Harold lift a cordless telephone from its bracket and settle down at the kitchen table.

'I'll get through, then pass it over,' he told Charles. 'It's an Ambleside number.'

Charles watched him pressing buttons on this new contraption. At Lulling's vicarage no such modern equipment was in use. A venerable instrument stood on the chest in the hall, and when it rang one simply hurried to it from the bedroom, the kitchen or the garden and announced oneself with as much breath as was left.

'Can I speak to Mr Wilberforce?' said Harold, and handed the telephone to Charles.

A woman was speaking. 'At work,' said the voice, 'but if it is urgent I could give you his number at the office, or I can leave a message for him.'

'Get the number,' whispered Harold.

'If you would be kind enough to give us his office number,' said the rector diffidently, 'if you think he will be free, of course. I should not like to interrupt any business matters he may be engaged upon, but it really is rather urgent.'

Harold was drumming his fingers on the table, but stopped as Charles wrote the number at the head of the letter in front of him.

'Most kind, most kind, Mrs Wilberforce,' he said. Something was said at the other end, and Charles's chubby face grew pink.

'I apologize, Mrs Er – er –' he said. 'And many thanks again.'

'Who was it?'

'His housekeeper. I didn't catch her name. Shall we try the office?'

'Certainly. I'll get it, shall I?'

'Please do. I don't think I have quite mastered it.'

He watched Harold as he tapped briskly at the buttons, then took the telephone from his hand.

'Is Mr Wilberforce free?' he began. 'My name is Charles Henstock, and I am the rector of Thrush Green. He wrote to me about some documents of his aunt's.'

There was a pause.

'He's coming,' Charles whispered excitedly. He held up a hand as a voice spoke at the other end.

'I must apologize for troubling you at work,' began the rector, but then became silent and attentive. 'That would be most kind. Yes, the post *can* be a little unreliable. In that case, perhaps after your meeting? For dinner, say? We can easily put you up overnight. I can't tell you how much this means to us. I will give you my telephone number, and look forward to hearing from you this evening.'

When Charles had finished he was smiling. Harold was fidgeting with impatience.

'Sounds a very sensible chap,' said Charles. 'He has to come to Ealing some time on business, and will bring the papers with him. He promises to deliver them to me personally, as he can come via Thrush Green. He doesn't seem to rely on the post.'

Harold forbore to remark that most people, less trusting than the good rector, felt the same.

'I shall know when he's coming this evening,' continued Charles. 'He is making arrangements, so I'll be in touch with you as soon as I've heard from him.'

'Marvellous!' said Harold. 'I can't wait to get my hands on

all this material. We shall have to find a very safe place to store it.'

'I've no doubt that this house would provide the best possible shelter,' said Charles, 'and the most loving care.'

'You can be assured of that,' agreed Harold.

When his wife Isobel returned from her visit to Sussex, Harold told her the great news even before she had put the kettle on for a reviving cup of tea.

Weary though she was from her long drive, she did her best to match his enthusiasm. 'What will you do with the letters?' she enquired.

'Put them in our safe,' he replied.

'No, I meant permanently. Will you give them to the county archives?'

Harold looked dismayed. 'I can't say I'd got that far.' A note of doubt became evident in his speech. 'I suppose that would be the *correct* thing to do, but I'm jolly well going to keep them here at Thrush Green for as long as I can.'

'And why not?' agreed Isobel, pouring boiling water into the teapot. 'After all, without you Thrush Green would have remained completely ignorant of Nathaniel.'

Harold carried the tea tray into the sitting-room, followed by Isobel. Outside the rain still fell relentlessly, but it was snug by the fire, and soon they would draw the curtains against the unkind world outside.

It was beginning to grow dark but the bronze statue of Harold's hero was discernible through the window. Drops dripped from the Bible which Nathaniel held before him, and there was a steady trickle from his frock-coat tails. An impertinent sparrow was perched upon his shining head, but Nathaniel continued to smile benignly upon the rain-lashed scene of his birth.

'Will you meet this Mr Wilberforce?' asked Isobel.

'I intend to,' replied Harold. 'He sounds a very public-spirited sort of chap. After all, most people would have thrown the stuff away, and not bothered to get in touch with the rector.'

'How did he know about the rector?'

'Well, the letters were addressed to this fellow Octavius Fennel who was rector here when Nathaniel went away, so Wilberforce simply wrote to the present rector of Thrush Green, arid our postman Willie Marchant took it up to Lulling, and that's that.'

'What excitement!'

'We shall have to have a celebration of some kind.'

Isobel refilled her husband's cup. 'Let's get the letters first,' she advised.

Winnie Bailey, on the other side of Thrush Green, did not see the rector hurry to his car through the driving rain to return to his vicarage a mile away in Lulling. Charles Henstock served several parishes, but he lived in a beautiful house close by the magnificent church of St John's in the little town, with his wife Dimity.

She had lived in Thrush Green for several years with her old friend Ella Bembridge, and the two spinsters had been very busy and happy. Dimity's marriage to the widowed rector left Ella alone at Thrush Green, but the two remained close friends and met often.

On this particular morning of portentous news, Ella had called at Winnie's to return a library book.

'Thought I'd better do it while I remembered,' she explained, when Winnie remonstrated with her about venturing forth in such weather. 'Don't want to let you in for a hefty fine.'

She followed Winnie into the kitchen and greeted Jenny who was chopping up onions.

'By the way, Jenny,' she added, 'did you go to Thrush Green school as a child?'

'I did indeed,' said Jenny.

'Then you know it's a hundred years old next year?'

'Never!' said Jenny.

'So there'll be some high jinks, I gather. I saw the headmaster at the newsagent's yesterday, and he told me.'

'I wonder what they'll do?' said Jenny, scraping the chopped onion into a neat pile with her knife.

'A party, I expect,' said Winnie. 'We'll probably have to make a cake.'

'I'm quite happy to make a cake,' replied Ella. 'Anything rather than sitting through a concert on those uncomfortable chairs.'

'Perhaps they'll have both,' said Jenny. 'A hundred years is quite something, isn't it? I wonder if Miss Watson and Miss Fogerty will come back for all the fun?'

'I'm sure they will,' said Ella. 'Mr Lester said as much yesterday. They taught here for so long.'

'I can see some excitement in our midst,' commented Winnie. 'Coffee, Ella?'

But she refused, saying that she had left a piece of gammon simmering, and by now it was probably splashing all over the stove.

She plunged homeward through the rain.

As the day ended, the rain began to die away, but little rivulets continued to trickle down the sides of the hill leading to the town of Lulling, and on roads around Thrush Green vast puddles caught the light of the rising moon.

Winnie Bailey, early in bed, was glad to rest. Although she had not ventured out for her usual afternoon walk, she felt as though she had been buffeted by the wind which had rattled round the house all day.

Tomorrow, she told herself, she would do some gardening and take a walk. It was time she went to see her old friend Dotty Harmer who lived near Lulling Woods some half-mile distant.

Ella Bembridge, a hundred yards from Winnie Bailey, was still up and about. She leant across the window-sill and breathed in the fragrance of wet earth. Across the green she could see the shape of the school with the school house beside it. She liked Alan Lester, the new headmaster, and his wife, but missed Dorothy Watson, the former head teacher, and her friend and colleague Agnes Fogerty.

Well, she hoped they would come to all the jollifications that appeared to be looming for next year.

The moon appeared briefly between ragged clouds, and Ella shut the window against the chill of a November night.

At the school house Alan Lester was carrying a tray bearing two mugs of hot milk and some digestive biscuits into the sitting-room, where his wife Margaret was busy counting stitches on her knitting needle.

'A hundred and four last time, and a hundred and six this,' she told her husband. 'I wonder which is right?'

'What's it supposed to be?' he enquired, putting down the tray.

'A hundred and four.'

'Forget the second count,' said Alan.

'I think I shall. Has it stopped raining?'

'Yes, and the wind's dropped. At least the children will be able to go out and play tomorrow.'

They sipped their milk in companionable silence, and half an hour later were in bed.

Next door Harold Shoosmith and his wife were also abed. Isobel fell asleep quickly, tired after her journey, but Harold was too excited by the prospect of seeing his hero's letters to follow his wife'e example.

He crept out of bed and went to look at the sleeping world of Thrush Green. Clouds scudded across the moon's face, but it was light enough to see Nathaniel Patten's figure on the grass before him.

What news! What a day! He remained at the window, relishing his happiness, until the winter's cold brought goose-pimples to his arms, and his feet grew stone-cold.

Sighing happily, he sought the comfort of his bed.

A mile away at Lulling vicarage, Charles Henstock, too, was sleepless beside his slumbering wife.

The expected telephone call had not come until almost ten o'clock, and the good rector had decided to ring Harold in the morning rather than at that late hour.

It seemed that Mr Wilberforce came about once a quarter to Ealing on business, and could bring the documents in about a month's time. Yes, he had said, he usually stayed overnight, and sometimes two nights, when he was down, and would be delighted to accept the rector's kind invitation.

They agreed a date together, and Charles was already making plans for Harold and Isobel to meet him.

It was all very satisfactory, thought Charles, as St John's church clock struck twelve silvery chimes. There would be no more chimes until seven the next morning, for the clock had been subdued to silence, by common consent, during the small hours.

Tomorrow, Charles told himself, he would have the pleasure of telling Harold all about it. He turned his head more comfortably into his pillow and fell asleep.

2. THE SEARCH BEGINS

The fact that Thrush Green school would soon be a hundred years old had not escaped the notice of Dorothy Watson and Agnes Fogerty, although they were far away.

The two friends had retired from teaching at Thrush Green some years earlier, and now shared a bungalow at Barton-on-Sea. Here they enjoyed the sea air, the gentle countryside around, new friends and, above all, each other's company. Dorothy, who had been the headmistress, took most of the decisions, but Agnes, who had been in charge of the infants' department, although acquiescent nine times out of ten, occasionally overruled her friend.

The subject of Thrush Green's anniversary had cropped up as the result of a telephone conversation the night before. Isobel Shoosmith rang frequently, for she missed her old neighbours and was particularly attached to little Agnes Fogerty, for they had attended the same teachers' training college many years before, and had always kept in touch.

It was Isobel who had said that Alan Lester was already thinking about a celebration at the school, and the two friends had naturally been much interested.

'No doubt we shall get an invitation,' announced Dorothy as they washed up the breakfast things. 'I must admit that I can't recall just when the school opened. Was it in the summer, do you think?'

'I have a feeling that it was earlier in the year,' said Agnes, twirling her teacloth inside a tumbler.

'I don't think you are right,' said Dorothy firmly.

'Maybe not,' agreed Agnes equably, 'but in any case it will be in the appropriate log book and Alan Lester can look it up.'

'Well, I only hope he does something suitable, and within the scope of the children and the school building. Some of these young men will try to be too ambitious. Do you remember that disastrous grammar school concert in Lulling where massed recorders waffled away at a piece by Haydn, and all at sixes and sevens?'

'I shall never forget it.'

Dorothy paused in her washing-up operations and gazed thoughtfully through the kitchen window above the sink. 'I wonder,' she mused, 'if it would be a good idea to have a word with Alan Lester. He might be glad of a little advice from an old hand.'

'It would be quite out of the question,' said Agnes. 'It is *his* school now, you know.'

Dorothy sighed. 'I suppose so. Nevertheless—'

Her voice trailed away, and Agnes, who knew her friend better than that lady knew herself, realized that the danger of Dorothy blundering into matters which were not her concern still hung over them.

As it happened, Alan Lester had temporarily shelved the matter of Thrush Green's celebrations.

The end of the winter term was looming, and Christmas with all its attendant distractions had to be faced before the anniversary year began.

He was a conscientious head teacher, and enjoyed the post he had taken up at Thrush Green some years earlier, although his first year had been fraught with anxiety about his wife

Margaret, whose health had never been robust, and who had taken to secret drinking with alarming consequences. This addiction she had bravely overcome, and now all went well, but there was never any alcohol in the Lesters' home, and Alan was extra careful of his wife's frailty.

He had taken over a well-run school from Dorothy Watson, and was wise enough to follow much the same paths, only gently introducing some of his more modern methods as time passed.

He also inherited Miss Robinson, a cheerful young woman, who took over the infants' department from Agnes Fogerty. The third member of staff was also young, only just out from college, and still trailing the clouds of child psychology, pastoral care, and the perils of damaging infant sensibilities, but the day-to-day reality of the classroom would soon clear those in time, Alan Lester surmised correctly. The three worked well together and the inhabitants of Thrush Green, whether parents of pupils or not, were proud of their school.

Alan Lester had no doubt that its hundredth birthday would be celebrated in fine style.

But meanwhile, there was Christmas . . .

But Harold Shoosmith had more urgent things than Christmas to occupy him.

The rector's invitation to dinner in mid-December to meet Robert Wilberforce was enthusiastically accepted by Harold and Isobel, and it was only a few hours later that Harold had been struck by a stupendous idea.

'Why not get in touch with Nathaniel's grandson again, or perhaps his wife and daughter?' he enthused to Isobel.

'But surely,' she pointed out, 'that man – Mulloy, wasn't it – was completely non-cooperative last time?'

Somewhat dashed, Harold was forced to agree. 'But his wife

was helpful. And Nathaniel's great-granddaughter must now be grown up. I wonder if they would consider it?'

It was quite clear to Isobel that her husband would cling to this idea as resolutely as a terrier with a rat. 'You should have a word with Charles,' she advised. 'I imagine you are thinking of getting these people an invitation to the dinner party. I think Dimity and Charles should be told about your scheme. If the Mulloys are coming from Wales, they would need to stay overnight.'

'You are quite right,' agreed Harold. 'I get carried away. I will see how Charles feels about it.'

Later that day he rang the rector, who said he would consult his wife.

'After all,' Charles said, 'it is Dimity who has to provide the meal, and I do just wonder if Wilberforce would be at all interested in meeting the Mulloys. In any case, I must say at the outset, Harold, that I utterly refuse to have that dissolute fellow we met in Wales at my table.'

'Fair enough,' said Harold. 'I didn't propose to approach him. But the little girl we met—'

'Dulcie,' said the rector.

'That's right! Named after Nathaniel's daughter, her grandmother. She might be available. Shall I try to find out? I'll report back, and you and Dimity can decide the next step.'

The rector agreed, unable to bring himself to discourage his enthusiastic friend, despite certain reservations about approaching the Mulloy ladies. Nathaniel Patten would have been a most welcome addition to a party at Lulling vicarage, but his descendants might not be such good company, thought Charles. He awaited developments.

Although it was some twenty years since the two men had been in touch with Nathaniel's descendants, Harold set about the task of tracing them again the next morning with his usual energy and common sense.

He remembered the name of the Welsh village, and found the number of the local post office. If anyone could tell him about the family, it would be the local postmaster or mistress.

A woman answered in a lilting Welsh voice. 'I have to tell you that Mrs Mulloy died two or three years ago, and we heard of her husband's death before that, but Miss Dulcie is in London. They moved up there about eight years since. Dulcie's doing well. She was always bright, you know.'

A vision of a diminutive child briskly cutting up cabbage with a fearsome kitchen knife returned to Harold over the years. Yes, he thought, she had looked a competent little thing even then.

'And you have her address?'

'That I have. Letters still come now and again. Reunions at the girls' grammar school and that. I send them on.'

'Could you let me have it? And her telephone number?'

There was the sound of rustling paper, then she spoke again. 'I've no telephone number for her, but this is her address.'

She read it carefully, repeating each line with much emphasis, to Harold's amusement.

The young lady lived in a flat in north London evidently.

'But she works in a big office in London. Insurance, I think, but I don't know that address. Is it urgent?'

'No, no indeed,' Harold assured her. 'A friend and I met her when she was a child, and it is simply a little family matter we thought she might like to know about.'

'Money, is it? Left to her, I mean?'

'No, nothing like that.'

'Pity. She could do with it, I don't doubt, in spite of this fine job she's got. But there, we could all do with some more, couldn't we?'

Harold agreed, thanked her warmly for her help, and went to tell Isobel.

At the time when Harold was intent on tracking down Dulcie Mulloy, great-granddaughter of his hero, Winnie Bailey had decided to call on her old friend Dotty Harmer who lived some half-mile away to the west.

She took with her some magazines and a pot of honey, food for mind and body. Not that Dotty's mind really needed stimulation; if anything it needed slowing down, thought Winnie, remembering the way Dotty flitted from subject to subject with the most extraordinary mental agility for one of her advanced years. Winnie had heard her hold forth on animal welfare (Dotty's chief concern), modern education, the deterioration in public speaking, the shortcomings of the Church of England, the proliferation of caterpillars in this year's cauliflowers, all within the space of five minutes.

Dotty's father had taught at Lulling Grammar School for many years, and the remembrance of his punishments still caused strong men of Lulling to blench.

His sons had left home as soon as they could, but Dotty, who had never married, kept house for him until he died. She admired his undoubted brilliance of mind, his high principles and his physical bravery. She had seen him tackle a runaway horse careering down the steep hill from Thrush Green to Lulling when he was in his sixties, whilst younger men stood gaping and too shocked to stir themselves to action.

On his death she had moved to a small cottage set among fields, where she had spent her time happily alone, surrounded by all kinds of animals from bantams to stray dogs and cats, not to mention goats for which she had a particular fondness, and two tortoises who were probably older than Dotty and to whom she bore a strong facial resemblance.

She delighted in collecting the harvest of the hedgerows and meadows and made preserves which she pressed upon her many friends with dire effect. 'Dotty's Collywobbles' was a local internal complaint known to Lulling and Thrush Green residents, and newcomers were warned about accepting Dotty's largesse.

Her contented solitude had to end when she became infirm. When her niece Connie met and married Kit, they decided to enlarge the cottage sympathetically rather than uproot Dotty and move somewhere bigger.

Winnie always enjoyed visiting Dotty. Her kitchen remained the same chaotic muddle she had always known. Connie, very wisely, had an adjoining kitchen, where the real business of cooking was done.

As Winnie crossed the green to take the path to Lulling Woods, she met Albert Piggott emerging from his cottage opposite the church.

'Nice day, Albert,' said Winnie, as he paused on his doorstep.

'Bound to rain later,' said Albeit morosely.

Typical of Albert, thought Winnie with some amusement. Nothing pleased the surly old scoundrel. He had been sexton of Thrush Green church and an occasional jobbing gardener to whomsoever would employ him, for as many years as Winnie could recall, but she had never seen him in a happy mood. He was lucky to have his buxom wife Nelly to look after him. She was the best cook in the district, and spent most of her time and energy in the kitchen of The Fuchsia Bush, a renowned tea-room in Lulling High Street, where her skills were much appreciated by her partner there, Mrs Peters.

'Well,' said Winnie, 'I hope the rain holds off until I get home again. I'm just off to see Miss Harmer.'

Albert's glum countenance lightened a little. He liked old Dotty. 'Ah!' he said, nodding.

Winnie moved on, leaving Albert still standing equidistant between the church and The Two Pheasants.

Which, wondered Winnie, taking the path through the fields, would Albert visit first?

She found Dotty at her kitchen table, not making chutney, jam or bottling some fearsome fungi she had come across on her travels, but plying a pen.

She rose to greet Winnie affectionately. 'Just in time,' she cried. 'How do you spell "benefited"? One "t" or two?'

'You've got me there,' confessed Winnie. 'I know if I'm not asked, but the same awful doubt arises as when one is asked if it's the sixteenth or seventeenth of the month. I think it must be one "t".'

'Good!' said Dotty. 'I'm just describing my father's gastro-enteritis.'

She held up an exercise book which had a shiny mottled cover. It brought back memories to Winnie of a science exercise book she had used as a schoolgirl. She could even recall the laboriously drawn illustration of a copper ball suspended over a tripod. Something to do with heat expansion, she remembered, through the mists of time.

'But what are you doing, Dotty?' she asked.

'I'm writing a biography of my father. So many people have memories of him, and I thought it would be so nice to have these recollections recorded. After all, he made a deep impression on his pupils.'

Physical as well as mental, thought Winnie, but forbore to comment.

'And I was just explaining how his gastroenteritis *benefited* from a draught of parsley and woundwort I used to make for him to drink last thing at night. As a matter of fact, I was wondering if I should include the recipe. Some readers might be grateful, don't you think?'

'It would certainly fill up half a page,' agreed Winnie diplomatically. 'You're bound to need a lot of material for a full-scale biography.'

'Oh, I don't envisage a really *long* book! Not Charles Dickens' length. Something more in the way of a *vignette*. A slim volume, you know. Which publisher, do you think, should have it? It might well be a bestseller. Several people have said they will buy a copy, and there are hundreds of libraries who will want copies, I'm sure.'

She patted the mottled cover lovingly as if it were one of her many pets.

'Of course, I could do a *separate* cookery book. I've dozens of recipes, and the interest in herbs and their beneficial properties has increased enormously lately.'

'Quite an idea,' said Winnie.

'And I could have something in hand for the publishers when they had got out the first book. I believe that most writers have another book waiting to follow on the first.' Dotty's eyes were bright with enthusiasm behind her spectacles.

Winnie changed the subject. 'There is an interesting article about Gerard the herbalist in this magazine,' she said, putting it on the table, 'and some splendid photographs of Blenheim. I thought you'd be interested.'

'Harold and Isobel took me there a month or two ago,' said Dotty. 'Fascinating place, though I found the architecture somewhat grandiose. But have you heard Harold's news about Nathaniel Patten?'

'No. Tell me more.'

'Betty Bell told me. I don't know what I'd do without Betty to keep me in touch.'

Betty Bell was the exuberant woman who did her best to keep Dotty's domestic conditions in order. She also worked at the Shoosmiths and was a source of much local information.

'Someone has found some letters written by Nathaniel, and sent word about them to Charles, and he wants Harold to see them.'

'How exciting!'

'Harold can't wait to read them. Betty says he's like a cat on hot bricks. Such a *cruel* expression if you dwell on it. I wonder why some people are so vindictive towards cats? That dreadful phrase about more ways of killing them than by choking them with cream, for instance. So *sadistic!*'

'Well, I'm delighted for Harold's sake,' said Winnie briskly.

She lifted the pot of honey from her basket, and put it by the magazines and Dotty's manuscript.

Dotty picked it up in her scrawny hands. She certainly could do with a little added flesh on those old bones, thought Winnie. Mentally, she had plenty of nourishment about her.

'How kind! So sweet and pure! A true natural comfort,' cried Dotty.

She put it down by the mottled exercise book, and patted the latter with proprietory affection again.

'I wonder if my little work will occasion as much pleasure one day,' she mused.

'I'm sure of it,' said Winnie. 'I shall leave you to carry on with your work.'

She saw herself out, and as she passed the kitchen window she saw that Dotty had taken up her pen again, and was immersed in her memories.

News of the existence of some letters written by Nathaniel Patten soon spread among the inhabitants of Thrush Green and Lulling.

Charles had told his wife Dimity about them, as a matter of course, and she, as a good clergyman's wife, had been as discreet as ever about the news. Harold and Isobel knew, of course, and were eagerly looking forward to meeting Robert Wilberforce and studying the letters he was about to bring to them.

But now, it seemed, everyone knew about this exciting find. How *did* the news get around so quickly, wondered Winnie as she retraced her steps?

It was like seed dispersal, she told herself, ancient memories of botany lessons stirred again by that glimpse of Dotty's exercise book so like her own Elementary Science notebook of years ago. Seeds were dispersed by wind, as in the case of thistledown, or by birds eating berries, or even by water. Winnie had some faint recollection of coconuts floating in Pacific seas and germinating on island shores.

Yes, it must be *wind* dispersal in this case. The news seemed to be airborne. It was unlikely that Harold had discussed the matter with Betty Bell, yet she knew. No doubt Albert Piggott knew as well, thought Winnie, catching sight of him wielding a besom broom by the church porch. Obviously he had already called at The Two Pheasants, for the door of the inn stood open hospitably, and his movements were unusually brisk.

She crossed the grass to her own house and found Jenny brushing down the stairs with considerably more vigour than Albert Piggott's efforts across the way.

She stopped when she saw Winnie. 'Rector's been in and says can he count on you to do the crib with Miss Bembridge and his wife as usual this Christmas? And have we got any jumble for the scouts, and don't forget they're collecting for the Deanery Christmas Bazaar's produce stall.'

'Good heavens!' cried Winnie. 'What a lot to remember!'

Jenny put down her brush. 'And talking of remembering, we're too late to post surface mail to Australia. Christmas things will have to be air mail now to your cousins.'

'It happens every year,' sighed Winnie.

'Mind you,' said Jenny kindly, 'you're still all right for America, and Europe's not so bad.'

'That's a change,' remarked Winnie tartly. 'Europe these days can be most awkward.'

She made her way to the kitchen to make coffee.

Over their steaming cups ten minutes later, Jenny spoke again. 'And there's more news. They've found some letters that Nathaniel Whatsit wrote years ago. Should be a thrill for Mr Shoosmith.'

Definitely wind dispersal thought Winnie, draining her cup.

Charles Henstock wrote to the address of Dulcie Mulloy which Harold had obtained from the obliging Welsh postmistress, but the days passed, and he had no reply.

Secretly, he rather hoped that the young lady would not be

able to come. Harold's enthusiasm swept one along, he mused. It would really be more circumspect just to entertain Robert Wilberforce, for Dulcie Mulloy was an unknown quantity and might not fit in with Harold and their new acquaintance. Harold seemed to think that she was a successful business woman, and Charles felt apprehensive. Would she be *bossy*? Would she be completely dismissive of Nathaniel's memory, as her deplorable father had been? Would she and Robert Wilberforce, who sounded such a quiet fellow on the telephone, take a dislike to each other? Would she demand Nathaniel's letters for herself as one of the family?

With such conjectures poor Charles tortured himself until Dimity, ever solicitous, asked him outright what was troubling him. After some hesitation Charles admitted that he had one or two qualms about the proposed dinner party.

Dimity, always practical, tried to put his mind at ease. 'Well, it's all arranged now, whether she comes or not, and really one must consider Harold's feelings. He would love to meet Dulcie, if that turns out to be possible, and both she and Mr Wilberforce are bound to be civilized people and won't make trouble under our roof. Do stop worrying, Charles dear. I'm sure it will be a very cheerful little party.'

'I do wish she would reply,' said Charles, only partially content.

'She may have moved from that address,' said Dimity, 'or be ill, or looking after someone else.'

'I realize that,' nodded Charles, 'but I just wish we had *heard*,' he added piteously.

That same evening the telephone rang as he and Dimity were finishing a modest supper of cauliflower cheese. Charles went to the hall to answer it, and took a long time in doing so.

Dimity stacked the dishes in the sink, set out two coffee cups, then settled herself at the kitchen table. She only hoped that the caller was not some troubled parishioner who was demanding Charles's immediate support and comfort. If so, she knew Charles would go at once to offer succour.

He returned beaming, and Dimity felt relief. At least he had not been called upon to take himself out into the dismal November night. She began to make the coffee.

'It was Dulcie Mulloy. Very apologetic for not getting in touch before, but she's been abroad on business. Hamburg or Frankfurt – one of those edible German towns – and she only got back today to find our letter.'

'And can she come?'

'She said she'd love to. She is going on to stay with friends in Wiltshire that night, but can come to dinner.'

'That is good news,' said Dimity, noticing the pleased expression on her husband's face.

'She sounds quite charming,' said Charles. 'Very soft voice. Very ladylike.'

Dimity hid her amusement. How often, these days, did you hear of anyone being 'ladylike'?

But then Charles was not of these days, she thought thankfully. 'So now you are happy?' she said, putting his coffee before him.

'I'm always happy with you,' said Charles.

3. A Memorable Evening

The Christmas street decorations began to go up in Lulling High Street at the start of December. Council men, perched on ladders, strung electric bulbs among the lime trees, and banners across the highway, causing even more traffic chaos than usual, and a number of distinctly unchristian comments from pedestrians stepping round bags of tools and coils of electric flex.

The shops were decking their windows with seasonal themes. Reindeer romped improbably round the electricity showrooms among refrigerators and ovens. Father Christmas sat on his sleigh amidst satin underwear and flimsy nightgowns in the window of Lulling's most prestigious draper's shop, and at the new florist's a gigantic silver and white arrangement of honesty, silvered pine cones and white Christmas roses evoked much admiration from the passers by.

At The Fuchsia Bush, Nelly Piggott and her staff had been busy preparing Christmas cakes and the results of their skill stood proudly in the window of that establishment. Fringed collars of scarlet and gold encircled the snowy wares, and red satin ribbon was draped tastefully across the windowpane to add even more attraction to the goods on display.

The scene at Thrush Green was much less colourful, although Mr Jones, the landlord of The Two Pheasants, had a Christmas tree standing in a tub outside the door of his hostelry, and this was decked with miniature light bulbs which made a brave show after dark.

But in all the houses around the green preparations were going on with increasing fervour as the December days were torn from the calendar.

Winnie Bailey was debating whether to send tights or hankies to her Australian cousins, mindful of postage expense.

Ella Bembridge was hand-blocking some material, which was destined to be made into ties for her unlucky male relations. The recipients, however, were quite used to these annual gifts, and passed them on, after a decent interval, to bazaars some distance from Thrush Green.

Nelly Piggott had cleared away the supper dishes, and was settling down at the table to write Christmas cards. Albert was next door at The Two Pheasants, and Nelly had time to sort robins from snowy churches, cats in bobble-hats from reindeer, in readiness for posting to friends and relations.

Joan and Edward Young, the local architect, who lived in the finest of all the Cotswold houses on the green, were planning a Christmas party for their schoolboy son, and Harold and Isobel Shoosmith were sorting out their bottles of wine and making a list for more.

But it was at Thrush Green school that the most intense of Christmas preparations were in force.

Alan Lester had decided to keep things as simple as possible. The decorating of the three classrooms would be left to the care of the teacher in charge, and Miss Robinson, across the playground in the infants' room, was already supervising the construction of yards of paperchains, a Christmas frieze to encircle the walls, and some individual cracker cases, destined for unsuspecting parents, and waiting to be filled with wrapped boiled sweets generously supplied by the enthusiastic Miss Robinson.

The paperchains and frieze were roaring ahead with little

difficulty, but the cracker cases were decidedly less simple than *The Teachers' World* diagram had shown, and infant tears had spotted many a piece of scarlet crêpe paper. In fact, Miss Robinson had almost decided to scrap that particular project and substitute nice plain squares of red paper which could be drawn up round the sweets and turned into a neat dolly bag with the aid of sensible and obliging wire tie closures.

The young probationer in the room next to Alan's had also embarked on an ambitious frieze showing angels with detachable wings which, in theory, fluttered in any light breeze available. It was a pretty notion on paper, but when transposed to practical hand work was far from successful. The Cotswold winds in winter are rough and rude, and at every opening of the classroom door the wings fell to the floor like confetti.

When Alan Lester discovered his assistant one playtime tearfully trying to stick back the recalcitrant wings, he suggested that these tiresome appendages should go into the wastepaper basket, and that wings could be added on each side of the figures quite effectively by drawing on the black background with white chalk.

'*Much* better,' agreed the girl, cheering up.

'You don't want to be too ambitious,' said Alan kindly.

'I thought of making some paper bells but they look rather tricky,' she admitted.

'What about paperchains?'

'But they *always* have paperchains!' protested the innovator.

'That's why they like them,' Alan assured her.

His own classroom was adorned with cardboard models of Father Christmas in his sleigh with rather weak-kneed reindeer pulling it. But beauty is in the eye of the beholder, and the children were enchanted with their efforts. Here, too, paperchains stretched overhead, and when a link occasionally gave way and there was a cascade of bright chains upon the heads beneath, it all added to the festive spirit.

The two older classes combined to practise carols, for it was in the school's tradition to take part in a carol service at St Andrew's on the green close by. The infants were exempt from this event, as excitement and nervousness had often brought tears, or worse, to the occasion, to the embarrassment of all present. They had a story read to them in the familiar comfort of their own classroom, while their elders fulfilled their public duties.

Alan Lester's two daughters were among his pupils, and were some of the keenest workers at the Christmas decorations. At home they continued their labours enthusiastically, and Alan found the schoolhouse as lavishly festooned in paperchains as the school itself.

'You know,' commented Alan to his wife Margaret when the little girls were safely in bed, 'I am a true lover of Christmas, but I do get a little tired of these ubiquitous paperchains.'

'Never mind,' said his wife consolingly. 'You know what Eeyore said about birthdays? "Here today, and gone tomorrow." Well, Christmas is much the same!'

'Ah!' replied Alan, 'but these things stay up until Twelfth Night. However, if the girls like them . . .'

'They do,' said Margaret; and there the matter was left.

Meanwhile, at the vicarage in Lulling, preparations for the dinner party were already going ahead.

Dimity, whose confidence in her ability to cook had grown since her marriage, was quite enjoying making lists of possible menus for the great occasion. She consulted Charles earnestly about his opinion, but always received the same unhelpful response: 'I'm sure that would be very nice, Dimity. Very nice indeed.'

Food meant little to Charles, and Dimity often wondered if he would patiently wade through a stewed boot or bread soaked in hot water if put before him. He would certainly not question such a meal, and probably compliment her when his plate was clean.

She remembered his angelic forbearance with the appalling meals his housekeeper had dished up, when Charles was a lone widower at Thrush Green years earlier. She and Ella had often taken pity on him, and invited him to lunch. He had always been excessively grateful, Dimity recalled, but now, after years of marriage and supplying him with meals, she wondered if perhaps she and Ella had been more satisfied then with their entertaining than their polite guest.

In the end Dimity had devised a main course which would survive in the oven should the guests be late in arriving. Chicken breasts in a creamy sauce in a casserole, accompanied by jacket potatoes, runner beans grown in the vicarage garden and taken from the freezer, and fresh carrots for a splash of colour should prove adequate. The problems of starters and puddings to augment the chicken kept Dimity engrossed happily for days beforehand.

Charles would be in charge of the wine throughout the evening, and here he took more interest and was quite knowledgeable. Dimity was content to leave things to him.

There would only be six at the table, but the plethora of dishes were to be tackled in the kitchen, while coffee was being taken in the vicarage's elegant drawing-room, by Mrs Allen, the stalwart daily help who usually came to give a hand with the housework on two mornings a week.

The warmest of the three spare bedrooms was to house Mr Wilberforce overnight, and Dimity was already planning the best arrangement of his bedside lighting and reading matter. With such domestic matters Dimity was happily occupied, while Charles thought only of the pleasure of seeing and handling the letters written so long ago by Nathaniel, and the diary kept by the Reverend Octavius Fennel who had once walked the streets of Lulling and Thrush Green to meet his parishioners, just as Charles himself did today.

At Thrush Green Harold Shoosmith looked forward to the evening with even greater excitement.

They were invited to the vicarage at seven o'clock to meet the other guests, and fortunately the night was clear. Fog had shrouded the Cotswolds for two days, causing traffic to progress at a walking pace in the towns, and making it necessary to have lights on all day in offices, shops and homes.

A breeze had sprung up in the late afternoon, swirling the mist away in long veils. By the time early dusk had fallen over Lulling, the Christmas lights were shining as brightly as ever, and there was general relief as the Shoosmiths set out.

The vicarage hall was also bright with extra polishing by Mrs Allen, a splendid azalea on the hall table, and a Christmas tree standing in the corner.

Dimity, flushed with her culinary efforts, greeted Isobel and Harold affectionately and ushered them into the drawing-room where Robert Wilberforce was standing.

He was tall and dark, aged about forty, and looked remarkably healthy, as if he might well take a brisk walk daily over his native fells. He was not handsome, Isobel decided as they were introduced, but attractive in a rugged open-air way. His voice was low with a north-country burr about it, and Harold, who would have liked the biggest villain on earth as carrier of Nathaniel Patten's letters, took to this amiable stranger at once.

The rector poured drinks and Robert's journey and the providential dispersal of the fog kept the conversation going. A briefcase stood by Robert's chair and Harold was longing to see it opened.

A few minutes later the door bell rang and Charles hastened to answer it.

'That will be Miss Mulloy,' cried Dimity. 'I do so hope she had an easy journey.'

The latest guest came in shyly, warmly greeted by Dimity who led her to the fire and began introductions.

She was a small woman with soft fair hair, and was clad in a coral-pink jersey suit. Harold thought how pretty she was,

this great-granddaughter of Nathaniel's, and remembered the gross unkempt man who was her father. Certainly this fragile-looking girl, whose small cold hand he held, did not take after her paternal parent.

Over their drinks she grew less shy and told them about her position in an insurance firm in the City, and how she went daily by Tube from her flat. Robert knew some of the directors of the company, and the conversation flowed easily.

Dimity hurried out to the kitchen to supervise the dishing-up operations, and while she was absent the rector said gently how sorry he was to learn that her mother had died, and how they remembered her kindness to them in Wales so long ago.

The girl looked down at the glass in her hand, and Charles wondered if he had been wrong to mention the subject, but Dulcie spoke calmly.

'We had two lovely years together in my flat,' she said, 'before she fell ill. I think they were the happiest years of both our lives.'

'So you live alone now?'

'At the moment. I suppose it would be sensible to get a friend to share with me, but I'm rather enjoying being on my own.'

'A lot to be said for it,' agreed Robert Wilberforce, 'but who looks after you?'

Dulcie looked bewildered. 'I look after myself.'

'But when you get home,' insisted Robert, 'who cooks a meal and so on?'

'Why, I do. It's no bother.'

Robert laughed. 'I suppose I'm spoilt. My housekeeper, Mrs Tanner, cooks and washes and does everything in the house for me. She's a Yorkshire lass and everything's kept at a pretty high standard. I have to leave muddy shoes in the porch.'

At this point, Dimity summoned them to the dining-room. Over the meal Charles enlarged on the excitement that had been engendered by Robert's gift of the letters to Thrush Green.

'Well, I must confess I had never heard of him until I went through my aunt's papers.'

'You're not the only one,' commented Harold. 'The name of Nathaniel Patten didn't seem to be known when I arrived here some years ago.'

'Now, come!' protested Charles. 'We knew he was buried in the churchyard, but we had no idea he was such a great man.'

'My Aunt Mary could have told you,' broke in Dulcie. 'She had a great many of his qualities, and she often quoted him to me as a good example. I'm afraid my father had no time for his memory.'

She said this with an apologetic smile towards Charles and Harold, and they realized, with some relief, that she had become quite reconciled to the memory of a far from satisfactory father.

Dimity's dinner was much enjoyed, although Harold was secretly so anxious to get hold of the contents of Robert's briefcase that he was scarcely aware of what was put before him.

When they were back at last in the drawing-room with coffee at their sides the great moment arrived, and Robert unclicked his case.

He handed a large envelope to Charles, and they all sat back to watch the rector open the treasure. A smaller envelope revealed a hardbacked diary, spotted with age, with a brittle silk ribbon marking a page.

'There's not a lot in the diary part,' said Robert, bending forward, 'but he seems to have kept his accounts in the latter half, and they look particularly interesting.'

'May I see?' burst from Harold, and Charles hastily handed the little volume to his anxious friend. A bundle of yellowing letters was next withdrawn from the envelope and Charles's chubby face grew pink with pleasure.

'I really feel,' he said, turning to Dulcie, 'that you should see them first as a direct descendant.'

But Dulcie would not hear of it, so Charles undid the string which held them, and looked at the first letter. The paper was brittle and so fragile that Dulcie thought of the paper burnt on a bonfire that turns to gossamer thinness before the wind shatters it.

The rector peered closely at the faded writing. 'It's dated 1892,' he told them. 'I can't see if it is January or July. He just puts "Jy". Let me see if I can make out the text.'

He adjusted the gold-rimmed spectacles on his snub nose, and cleared his throat.

It is now almost eight months since I said farewell to you at Bristol, and I write to tell you of the safety of our journey, and the beginnings of my endeavours which, with God's help and your prayers and inestimable support, I trust will be successful.

I have not yet met Dr Maurice as he is ministering to sufferers at a settlement up-river, but kind messages were waiting here from him on my arrival.

My faithful servant, already dedicated to Christ, awaits the conclusion of this letter, and will take it downstream some thirty miles to our nearest township where (Deo volente) it will go by the next ship to England.

My prayers, my thanks, and my whole heart go with this letter to one whose faith and bounty have inspired my life.

The rector's voice was husky with emotion as he read the words, written so long ago in the cruel heat of Africa, to one long dead. Both writer and first reader had loved Thrush Green, thought Charles, as he and the local friends with him did now.

There was a short silence, then Robert Wilberforce spoke. 'I find that very moving,' he said. 'And I think the date must be January. If you look in Octavius's diary you will see that he notes that a letter from Nathaniel arrived that summer. I imagine that fits.'

The rest of the company were as moved as Robert was, and longed to hear more.

'I shall spread them out,' decided Charles, 'on this side table, so that we can all see them easily. Somehow I don't think they'll stand much handling.'

They all helped to clear a space, and soon the fragile pages lay open to their gaze.

After some time, Dimity recalled them to the present by offering more coffee, and the company moved back to their chairs by the fire.

'They are not all dated,' said Harold. 'I wonder if we can get them into chronological order.'

'That's where the diary helps,' Robert told him. 'As far as I could make out, Octavius supplied the funds for this venture, and he seems to have put regular sums into an account at Coutts bank to support the mission.'

'But I don't think Nathaniel was backed by the Church,' said Charles. 'I wonder why Octavius was so generous? I know from records that he was a bachelor and a rich man, but it seems odd that as a churchman he should give so much to Nathaniel.'

'Reading between the lines,' replied Robert, 'I think he looked upon Nathaniel as a son. He mentions several times in the diary his sorrow that Nathaniel refused to take Holy Orders. Evidently the young man could not believe in all the tenets of the church, evangelical soul that he was, but had this burning missionary zeal with which Octavius had to be content.'

'We must try to find out more about Octavius,' mused Charles. 'He sounds a remarkable man.'

'There is possibly a full obituary in the back numbers of local papers,' said Harold. 'I'll look into it, shall I?'

And so it was agreed. Later the papers were carefully packed into a large file from the rector's study to save them from being folded again, and they were given into the welcoming hands of Harold Shoosmith.

'This must be a particularly important occasion for you,' said Charles kindly to Dulcie. 'You had a wonderful forebear.'

'I know,' replied the girl. 'I only wish my mother and my Aunt Mary were alive to rejoice with me. Aunt Mary spoke of him often, although of course she had never met him.' She looked at the clock. 'I'm afraid I ought to be on my way. My friends expect me soon after ten. It's been such a wonderful evening for me.'

She said goodbye to the Shoosmiths, then to Robert Wilberforce.

'I hope we shall meet again,' he said. 'Do you ever visit the Lake District?'

'I may be going there next spring,' she told him, 'to see old friends.'

'Then perhaps you would come and have lunch with me?'

'I should very much like to.'

She went out to the car, accompanied by Charles and Dimity.

'It's a fine clear night,' said Charles, when they returned to warm their hands at the fire. 'What a charming girl she is.'

'Has she far to go?' asked Robert.

'Only half an hour's drive, she said.'

'I never like the idea of women driving alone after dark,' said

Robert. 'A friend of mine was foolish enough to give a wretched fellow a lift, and he knocked her about pretty badly.'

'Oh, I don't think Dulcie Mulloy would be so silly,' said Isobel comfortingly. 'I thought she seemed a very sensible young woman, and obviously she was as thrilled as we all are with your wonderful discovery.'

'It's been an amazing evening,' agreed Harold. 'A thousand thanks for everything,' he added, kissing Dimity's cheek.

'And now we must think about bed,' said Dimity when Charles returned from seeing them off. 'I'm sure you must be tired after a day's business, and then all this excitement.'

'I have enjoyed every minute,' Robert assured her.

'What nice old-fashioned manners Robert Wilberforce has,' commented Isobel, as they drove down Lulling High Street towards home. 'I'm sure there aren't many men these days who worry about women driving alone after dark.'

'I do about you,' Harold told her. 'You're quite soft-hearted enough to give some plausible bounder a lift.'

Isobel seemed not to hear. She was immersed in her own thoughts. 'Perhaps he's slightly smitten,' she said dreamily.

'Oh, rubbish!' said Harold, swinging round Thrush Green. 'There was absolutely no sign of any nonsense like that. You women are all alike, scenting romance where there's nothing.'

'Maybe,' agreed Isobel equably.

4 · HAROLD IS ON THE TRAIL

The last day of the term at Thrush Green school had gone without a hitch. The older children, hair brushed and coats neatly buttoned against the cold of the Cotswold winds outside and the Victorian chill of St Andrew's interior, filed decorously into their pews at the front of the church, and took part in the carol service conducted by the Reverend Charles Henstock.

The crib glowed at the side of the chancel steps, and piles of ivy and other evergreens waited in readiness for the ladies of the parish to put the final touches to the Christmas decorations in the next day or two.

At the school, the paperchains and friezes had been taken down and put into bin liners to await recycling. In the denuded infants' classroom, the last hours of term were devoted to stories, singing and such age-old games as 'I spy' which needed no apparatus, while their elders were at the carol service.

Alan Lester felt very proud of his little flock as they filed into the church, and ignored Albert Piggott who had stationed himself by the porch in order to cast a malevolent eye on those who omitted to use the doormat with suitable energy.

Margaret Lester sat by her husband, and he thought how lucky he was to have a wife who was healthy again, and a job which gave him satisfaction. As he looked fondly at the glossy

43

heads of Kate and Alison Lester, just in front of their parents, Alan counted himself a fortunate man indeed.

Winnie Bailey had enjoyed setting up the crib at the chancel steps on the day before the carol service. She had performed this pleasant duty for more years than she could remember, usually in the company of Ella Bembridge and Dimity, but sometimes alone.

To tell the truth, she really preferred to go about her task alone. There was something very soothing about working in the solitude of the church. It was not an old building, as churches go. It did not have the ancient splendour of St John's in Lulling, a wool church of dignity and beauty as great as those at Burford or Lechlade or Fairford not very far away. St Andrew's was Victorian with over-elaborate stained-glass windows, a fussy reredos and some deplorable encaustic tiles which succeeded in distracting the attention of communicants as they knelt at the altar rail.

But its smallness gave it a homeliness which Thrush Green folk liked, and in much the same way that Winnie had become accustomed to – even fond of – the crack in her bedroom ceiling, and the wardrobe door which swung open at odd times, so she felt affection for the shortcomings of her church's fabric.

On this particular occasion she was not alone for long. She had relished her solitary silence for a quarter of an hour, and felt refreshed in spirit, when Ella and Dimity joined her.

There was not a great deal to do, for the ladies were used to setting up the crib, making sure that the dim electric bulb which lit it was safely away from straw and hangings, and that the doll-child was easily visible to those passing the crib.

After ten minutes or so Ella returned from the vestry with dustpan and brush, and began to tidy up the wisps of straw and greenery.

'Perishing cold out,' she remarked to her companions, in what Winnie felt was much too loud a voice for a sacred place. At least, she told herself charitably, Ella was not smoking – a laudable tribute to holiness.

'I've put the kettle ready,' went on Ella, brushing lustily. 'Need a cuppa after this. Bit dusty in here, isn't it? And that brass lectern could do with a rub.'

'Mrs Bates is going to do the brights ready for the carol service,' explained Dimity, 'and yes, please, I'm sure we could both do with tea.'

Half an hour later, the three friends sat by Ella's fire enjoying tea and anchovy toast, and the talk was of Harold Shoosmith's delight over the discovery of Nathaniel's letters.

'He's going along to the newspaper people,' Dimity told them, 'to see if he can find out more about Nathaniel, and about Octavius Fennel, too. Everyone knew he was a good man, but it doesn't seem to be generally known how much he did for Nathaniel out in Africa.'

'The Lovelock girls might know,' said Ella.

'The Lovelocks?' queried Dimity. 'But even they wouldn't remember Octavius!'

The Lovelock girls were now, all three of them, around eighty years old, and lived in a pretty Georgian house in Lulling High Street, next door to The Fuchsia Bush. They had lived there all their lives, and were renowned for their excessive gentility and parsimony. Friends invited to a meal there usually stoked up beforehand with a slice of cake or a sandwich, whilst getting ready. Such a prerequisite of lunch at the Lovelocks' might not fully compensate for the paucity of the provender supplied but at least it mitigated the noise of tummy-rumbles.

'Oh, not the girls themselves,' said Ella, beginning to roll one of her untidy cigarettes, 'but I think their father knew Octavius Fennel. I'm sure I've heard them speak of him.'

There was a gasp from Winnie, and she replaced her cup on its saucer with a great clatter. She fell back in the chair with her eyes closed.

Dimity and Ella sprang to her side, Ella's cigarette-making equipment crashing into the hearth.

'Winnie, Winnie! What is it?'

After a few deep breaths, Winnie opened her eyes. 'Sorry about that. Better now,' she whispered.

'But what's hurting you? Shall I get John Lovell?'

'Heavens, no!' said Winnie, struggling upright. 'I'm fine now. I just occasionally get this pain on my right side. It goes within a minute. Nothing to worry a doctor about.'

'I think it is,' said Dimity roundly. 'Suppose you were taken ill in the street? Crossing the road? Going down steps, say?'

Winnie laughed tremulously. 'Don't worry about it. If it does get worse I will have a word with John, but I really can't face going back and forth to the county hospital for tests and things. Particularly just before Christmas.'

'Well, let me give you more tea. That must be cold.'

Winnie accepted the fresh cup, and conversation was resumed, but the subject of the Lovelock girls' father and his friendship with Octavius was forgotten.

Ella insisted on accompanying Winnie on the few yards' walk to her own home, and when Winnie was safely back in her armchair, she spoke to Jenny before she left.

'I know,' said Jenny soberly. 'I'm watching things, don't you worry, and if she gets many more of these spasms I'm telling Dr Lovell myself, come what may!'

A little easier in her mind about her old friend, Ella returned home.

Meanwhile, Harold had been tireless in his researches.

The editor of the local paper let him go through the files for 1912 when Octavius Fennel had died, but after a short and rather flowery obituary, the account of the actual funeral was taken up largely by a list of local dignitaries attending the service.

The county paper was more helpful, mentioning the generosity of the deceased and in particular his interest in missionary work. To Harold's great joy, Nathaniel Patten was mentioned and the date 1892 given as the year when his African mission settlement was officially opened.

Hot on the trail, Harold ploughed his way zealously through the weekly issues for that year, but was beginning to despair of finding any notice of Nathaniel's mission. By the time he had turned over the yellowing and musty pages of the summer weeks of 1892 showing photographs of ladies in ankle-length skirts and unwieldy hats at garden parties, race meetings, fetes and the like, he was almost ready to give up.

However, he determined to struggle on, and noted the change of attire in the ladies' fashions as the shooting season began. Wild duck, partridge, grouse, snipe, teal, hares and geese, all it seemed should be wary of men with guns as autumn loomed, and the silk skirts changed to tweed and the pale kid boots to glossy leather.

On 1 October, Harold read, pheasants, too, would have to watch out, and the issue of 26 October gave not only a fearsome photograph of a score of tweed-clad gentlemen sitting behind rows of birds' corpses, but also a short paragraph saying that word had been received by the Reverend Octavius Fennel from Mr Nathaniel Patten that the latter's mission station and school had been officially declared open on 1 October.

Harold leafed through the rest of that year's copy, but there was nothing more to interest him.

He shut the great book, sneezed as the dust of ages began to settle, and sat back well content.

October the first 1892!

Excitement engulfed him. Why, next year it would be a hundred years since that great day! Here was a sound reason for rejoicing, he told himself.

He must get in touch with Charles at once.

This certainly called for a special celebration at Thrush Green.

The news that Winnie Bailey's health was not quite as it should be soon flashed around Thrush Green.

Naturally, Winnie's uncomfortable twinges at Ella's were translated into more dramatic form.

Albert Piggott told his old friend Percy Hodge that she had been 'took bad with the gastric', and he had seen her being helped back to her own home by Ella Bembridge.

Betty Bell told the Shoosmiths that Mrs Bailey had 'had a turn', much to their dismay.

Mr Jones of The Two Pheasants, usually the soul of discretion in his capacity as local landlord, rashly said that it was no wonder poor old Mrs Bailey had caught a chill working in that church which was as cold as the tomb. Albert Piggott, within earshot, took umbrage at this slight on his efficiency as church caretaker, and stalked out, but not before he had drained the last of his half-pint.

Winnie, of course, knew nothing of these rumours which were floating about, and as she appeared as healthy as ever to her friends, they began to think that their informants had been over-egging the pudding as usual, and indulging in the common practice of gross exaggeration.

But Isobel Shoosmith, on her way to the postbox on the corner of Thrush Green, did ask Ella, on the same errand, if Winnie was really in good health.

Ella looked troubled. 'She makes very light of it, but she had a nasty spasm after we'd been doing the crib. Mind you, it was devilish cold in there. May have been that, of course, but I was just telling her about Octavius Fennel when she keeled over.'

'Has she seen John Lovell?'

'She's dead against it, but I reckon Jenny will fetch him pretty swiftly if she sees any symptoms. Winnie says the pain is only momentary, and nothing to worry about.'

'It worries *me*,' responded Isobel, dropping her bundle of envelopes into the box. 'I wonder if I ought to call?'

'I shouldn't,' advised Ella. 'Winnie's got plenty of sense, and if she gets any more pain she'll have a word with John.'

The ladies parted, and Isobel crossed the green to her home. Concern for Winnie occupied the larger part of her mind, but a phrase of Ella's niggled in one corner: 'I was just telling her about Octavius Fennel.' That would interest Harold, she knew.

She quickened her pace to tell her husband that Ella seemed to have something to add to his researches.

As she guessed, Harold was greatly intrigued and was about to hasten across to Ella's house, but was restrained by his wife.

'She was making for Nidden,' she told him. 'Do be patient. Give her a ring later.'

And with that Harold had to be content.

As for Winnie Bailey herself, all unsuspecting of the rumours flying around the neighbourhood, she was busy with her Christmas arrangements, in common with the rest of the community. She was honest enough to admit secretly to feeling tired and uneasy, but was determined to postpone any visits to the doctor until the festivities were over.

Her nephew Richard, his wife and two young children were coming to lunch on Boxing Day, and she and Jenny had planned to spend Christmas Day quietly together.

It was at times like this that Winnie realized how old she was getting. In the old days, a visit from Richard and his family would have been taken in her stride. Now she faced the fact that the extra work, the noise of two small children, the entertainment of her guests and the general disruption of her usual ordered routine all combined to dismay her.

Two days before Christmas Richard telephoned to tell her that the older child was in bed with measles, and the younger one seemed to be sickening for it. They were all terribly sorry, but their visit would have to be postponed.

Winnie was genuinely sad to hear the news, and said so, but was rather ashamed, as she put down the receiver, at the relief which flooded her.

A stab of pain made her sit down for a few minutes before she went to apprise Jenny about the change of plan.

'Well, I'm sorry for the poor mites,' said Jenny forthrightly, 'but to my mind it's a blessing in disguise for you just now.'

Harold's call to Ella had resulted in his being told that it was the Lovelocks who might know more about the deceased rector of Thrush Green; she herself knew nothing.

'You can't possibly go down to the Lovelocks, pen and pad in hand, on Christmas Eve,' Isobel told him. 'Do be sensible. All this has waited for a century. A few more days won't hurt.'

With commendable self-control Harold put aside his researches and joined in the celebration of Christmas with the rest of his neighbours, but before the year was out he rang the Misses Lovelocks' house, and was lucky enough to get the youngest one, Violet, at the other end of the line. Violet, although almost eighty, was rather more practical than her sisters, and her memory was decidedly better.

'I'm sure we have some papers of Papa's about Octavius Fennel, but I have a funny feeling that we got one of the young men from the choir to put a trunkful of that sort of thing in the loft. I will check with Ada and Bertha and ring you back.'

For the next hour Harold paced about the house within earshot of the telephone, doing his best to be patient.

Just as he and Isobel and Betty Bell, their daily help, were sitting down to their morning coffee in the kitchen, Violet Lovelock rang him.

'Yes, indeed. Bertha clearly remembers the trunk going up into the loft. And I have recalled the article that Papa wrote. It was one of a series about local people who had contributed to Lulling and Thrush Green in one way or another. Quite short, you understand. I believe the series first appeared in the church magazine, and Papa had them put together in a little leaflet.'

'Wonderful!' cried Harold. 'When may I fetch them?'

'Well, today we are turning out the spare room, and

tomorrow is bathroom-cleaning day, so what about Friday morning?'

Harold agreed readily. Secretly he wondered why the attentions to the Lovelocks' spare bedroom and bathroom forbade his picking up a leaflet from the ladies, but Violet's further explanation threw some light on the matter.

'I'm afraid we'll have to send you up into the loft to fetch the papers,' said Violet. 'We are now past coping with the little folding ladder.'

'No bother at all,' Harold assured her. 'I will look forward to seeing you at about ten, if that is convenient?'

'Perfectly,' said Violet, and rang off.

Charles Henstock, of course, had been kept informed of every step taken by Harold in his quest for details about Nathaniel and Octavius. The discovery of a firm date for the official opening of Nathaniel's mission gave both men great satisfaction and they were in entire agreement that something must be done to note the occasion in October next.

'I hope it won't clash with the school's centenary,' Charles said. 'I know that Alan Lester is keen to mark that. It's quite extraordinary how one's calendar fills up for months in advance, what with church festivals, and visiting clergy, and the dentist.'

'I don't have to worry too much about your first two,' admitted Harold, 'but the dentist certainly seems to figure in my diary far too frequently.'

'By the way,' continued Charles, 'we had a charming letter from Robert Wilberforce after his visit. He hopes that we will see him if ever we go his way. And he wanted Dulcie Mulloy's telephone number. I think he means to get in touch when he comes south next time.'

'Good!' said Harold. Could Isobel be right about

Wilberforce's interest in Nathaniel's descendant, he wondered? He dismissed the thought immediately. He was getting as bad as the rest of Thrush Green!

Friday came at last and Harold set out for Lulling High Street on foot. He carried with him a small case, notepad and pen.

'You look as though you are going for the weekend,' Isobel said.

'Well, heaven knows how much stuff I may find in that loft. I'm going prepared.'

He was greeted effusively by the three sisters who fluttered about him, pressing him to take coffee with them.

Harold managed to excuse himself, and was taken up two flights of stairs by Violet to what must once have been the servants' quarters. On the landing he espied a trap door above him which gave access to the loft and, he hoped, the treasure he was seeking.

Violet showed him how it opened and let down a metal

ladder. It looked remarkably wobbly to Harold, who was a large and heavy man, but he hoped for the best. Violet pressed a light switch on the landing wall, and a dim glow filled the square above their heads.

'Now, will you be all right?' asked Violet. 'There is a torch up there, I believe, though the battery may have gone. And I hope you don't mind mice. We hear them scampering about at night, dear little things. We none of us has the heart to trap them.'

She scurried away and Harold mounted the steps gingerly. He was relieved to find that the entire loft floor was boarded, and stood for a few moments trying to get accustomed to the dim light.

The sight that met his eyes was a revelation. The place was crammed with Victorian and Edwardian relics which would have delighted an antique dealer's heart. There were two enormous hip baths, three wooden towel rails, and a fireguard which had probably been in use some seventy or eighty years earlier in the girls' nursery. There were several dismantled iron bedsteads stacked against one wall, the legacy probably of servants long-dead, and a pile of circular hat boxes towering over a wicker chair with a dilapidated cushion showing signs of mouse occupancy.

Tennis racquets of antique design, skating boots, skis and a wooden sledge were propped in one corner beside a box of toys. In it Harold saw a diabolo set, a Russian egg, several jigsaw puzzles, a clockwork train, and a dolls' teaset. Hard by stood a dusty dolls' house, a replica of the one in which he now stood, down to the three front doorsteps and the brass knocker.

The Misses Lovelock must have been very fortunate little girls, thought Harold, stepping past these relics to half a dozen trunks which occupied the main part of the floor space.

To his relief, he saw that each bore a label written in a fair copperplate style, but faded and grimy with years. The largest bore the inscription 'APPARATUS – PHOTOGRAPHY AND ASTRONOMY'. The next in size said 'MAMA'S, AND OTHER FAMILY PICTURES'.

Harold turned his attention to the smallest case of the collection, a brown tin object bearing a label which seemed hopeful: 'PERSONAL PAPERS'.

The little trunk was unlocked, but the lid was difficult to lift.

When at last he had forced it open, Harold saw neatly packed bundles of letters, notebooks and some cardboard-covered pamphlets. He tackled these first, squatting on the dusty floor, peering closely in the dim light from the naked electric bulb above him. The torch, as Violet had indicated, was useless, and Harold intended to take it down with him when he descended.

The bundle of leaflets was tied with fine string, and they appeared to be written either by the Lovelocks' father himself or by some of his friends.

Harold turned them in his now filthy hands. They dealt with such subjects as 'Spirit Manifestations', 'Electrical Phenomena', 'Scientific Experiments' and 'Astronomical Data'. He was almost at the end of the collection when he came across one with the title 'Local Benefactors' and his heart leapt. Could this be the series which first appeared in the local parish magazine?

He stood up to get nearer to the light, and studied the index. Yes, here was something! 'The Reverend Octavius Fennel 1842–1912.'

The print was small and Harold had difficulty in reading it. He put it aside with the torch, and delved again into the papers. After an hour's search, he decided that this was really all that was relevant to his present endeavours, and he closed the lid, looked once more upon the dusty quietness of long ago, and retraced his steps.

'I am so very grateful,' he told Violet, as he washed the grime of ages from his hands at the kitchen sink. 'I will let you have this back as soon as I have copied out the important pieces, and I will also put a new battery in the torch, as a very small thank-you.'

He was in buoyant mood as he climbed the hill to Thrush Green. To be sure, the case he carried had only one small leaflet, and an ancient torch to keep it company, but Harold foresaw many happy hours ahead with this treasure from the Lovelocks' attic.

5. NEW LIGHT ON OLD TIMES

The first days of the New Year were mild and still. The naked trees stood motionless against a grey sky, and the hedgerows were spangled with drops from morn until evening.

In the gardens a few hardy flowers showed a little colour. Tough marigolds, brave pansies and here and there a pink, all somewhat bedraggled, nevertheless were tattered reminders of the summer long past.

Bright berries of pyracantha and cotoneaster glowed against the Cotswold stone, providing cheer for passers by and the hungry birds.

Indoors bowls of hyacinths and tulips gave hope of spring to come, sharing the tables and windowsills with the azaleas and poinsettias of Christmas.

It was a time to relish one's home. In the dark of the year, when curtains were drawn between four and five, and the long evening stretched ahead, the people of Thrush Green turned to their fires, books, knitting, needlework and, sometimes, television to amuse themselves. Domestic comforts became doubly precious: a warm bed, a hot drink, the snugness of curtains shut against the night's chill, all brought comfort in the dismal days of January.

Even Charles Henstock, who thought little about creature comforts, enjoyed these simple pleasures at Lulling vicarage, and occasionally thought about his former house at Thrush

Green which had been burnt down some years earlier. On that site there were now some homes for old people, one-storey pleasant places designed by Edward Young, the local architect.

Edward had always thought that Thrush Green rectory was an abomination, and had pitied Charles and Dimity, obliged to live in a tall bleak house entirely out of keeping with the Cotswold architecture around it. It faced north-east, and the front door opened on to a long passage which ran the length of the house forming a wicked wind-tunnel whenever one or the other door was opened. The ceilings were lofty, the windows badly fitting, there was no central heating and, even in summer, the interior was chilly.

When at last it vanished and the ashes and debris had gone, and Dimity and Charles had moved to Lulling vicarage, no one was more delighted than Edward; and to be asked to design the new buildings to take its place gave him enormous satisfaction.

Phoenix-like, the present homes had risen from the ashes, and everyone, even dear uncomplaining Charles who had grieved at the loss of his old home, agreed that Thrush Green had been much improved by Edward's endeavours.

It was at the old people's home, called Rectory Cottages in tribute to the former residence, that a coffee morning was held on one of the quiet cold days of January.

Thrush Green was particularly fond of coffee mornings to raise funds for whichever good cause was in need. Usually the posters proclaimed that those perennials, the church roof or the organ, were pleading for help. But sometimes the posters exhorted all folk of good will to save the children, or rain forests or whales.

On the whole these occasions were looked upon as a pleasant way of meeting friends and catching up with the local gossip, both laudable and necessary in a small community. The aim of raising money really took a lesser place of importance, although when the proceeds were counted, among the unwashed coffee cups and cake plates when the public had departed, it was usually found that the local good causes – Church Roof and/or Organ Fund – did rather better than Ethiopian Famine or Brazilian Earthquake.

'Which really,' said Winnie Bailey, seated in the warden's office at Rectory Cottages, 'is as it should be, I suppose. After all, charity should begin at home, and although we see all the dreadful things that are happening worldwide on telly, it's not quite the same as hearing the organ wheezing badly at Matins or watching a steady drip in the chancel.'

Jane Cartwright, the warden, agreed. 'I make it sixteen pounds forty-five,' she said, dropping piles of coins into plastic bags. 'That's all from the Bring and Buy stall. Nelly Piggott's seed cakes accounted for half that.'

'I can't understand this revival of popularity, for *seed cake*,' mused Winnie. 'Frankly, I find it abhorrent.'

'All my old dears love it,' Jane told her. 'Takes them back to their childhood.' She turned again to her accounts, brow furrowed. 'So this can be added to the raffle money. That brought in five pounds and four pence, though how we managed to get *four pence* when the tickets were ten pence each, I can't imagine.'

'Poor sight,' said Winnie kindly. 'Mistaking a two-pence piece for a ten-pence one.'

'I thought it was uncommonly generous of the Lovelocks to give that rather nice cushion as a prize. I mean, it's usually impossible to get them to part with anything.'

'They probably disliked it,' replied Winnie. 'As a matter of fact, I gave it to them last Christmas.'

'Oh dear,' cried Jane, 'I hope you don't mind?'

'Not in the least. I'm all in favour of recycling. Actually, the tray I put in was one they had given me years ago, so I suppose we are quits.'

The two ladies put the proceeds into a cash box ready for the bank, and Jane helped Winnie into her coat.

Winnie suddenly gave a little cry, rocked unsteadily, then sat down on the chair she had just vacated. Her face was white, her eyes screwed up in pain.

Jane, who had been a nurse, loosened the fastening of the coat she had just put on, and took hold of Winnie's hand.

'I'll ring the doctor,' she said.

'No,' gasped Winnie. 'Don't bother him now. In any case, he's probably on his rounds.'

'What is it? Has this happened before?'

'Too often for my liking,' confessed Winnie. 'That's the second time within twelve hours.'

'You simply must see John Lovell,' urged Jane.

'I shall go this evening,' Winnie promised her. 'I've been putting it off for weeks. They say that doctors' relations are always the most procrastinating, but I really will go tonight.'

'I hope it isn't anything you've eaten here,' said Jane, much perturbed.

'I assure you it wasn't seed cake,' replied Winnie. 'And now I'm quite all right again, and will go home.'

But Jane insisted on taking her the short distance to her gate, before returning, very worried, to her warden's duties.

Later that day Winnie submitted to John Lovell's probings and pressings and innumerable questions.

'I'm going to send you on to Dickie's,' he told her, naming St Richard's, the large county hospital. 'You'll need X-rays and some pretty painless tests, and then you'll probably be forwarded quite quickly to the consultant, Carter. I know him well.'

'Is he good?' asked Winnie nervously.

'Good? Of course, he's good,' responded John Lovell. 'He's a St Thomas's man!'

As John Lovell was himself a St Thomas's man, Winnie said no more.

'It sounds like the gall bladder,' said the doctor. 'Much easier to cope with these days. Very often no surgery is needed at all. I'll give you a prescription, and just cut out fat in your diet. I'll see that you get looked at quite quickly.'

'And you think I may not need surgery? I must admit that I have a horror of the knife.'

'Now don't worry. The chances are that if there are any stones there they can be dispersed, and if it comes to surgery Philip Paterson is the real expert at Dickie's, and he's a St Thomas's man, too. You'll be in safe hands.'

'Well,' said Jenny when Winnie returned, 'what did Dr Lovell say?'

Winnie told her.

'Are there any other doctors at Dickie's? I mean, who haven't trained at St Thomas's?'

'Not worth mentioning, according to John Lovell,' Winnie said.

Now that term was well on the way, Alan Lester set about looking for more details about the opening of Thrush Green school in 1892.

Unlike his neighbour, Harold Shoosmith, he did not have to search through contemporary local newspapers for his researches. Three stout log books, with mottled leather-edged covers, were carefully stored in the bottom drawer of his school desk, and in the oldest of these Alan found all that he needed.

The first entry was for 15 August, inscribed in a firm copper-plate hand. The ink had turned brown with age but the entry was clear:

> *Harvest now safely garnered, so that pupils could be*
> *admitted.*
> *Sixty-two enrolled. Some twenty still hop-picking in*
> *Hampshire, and returning before the month's end.*
> *Miss Mackintosh in charge of Infants. Miss Brown in*
> *charge of Juniors. Headmaster in charge of top standards.*
> *School assembled in the playground as weather fine, and*
> *then marched into Prayers.*
> *Text today: 'Be obedient to those set over you.'*

And a very timely text too, thought Alan Lester, for the first day of a new school!

He turned the pages, and soon found a lengthy account of the official opening, which took place on 20 September in the presence of a goodly gathering. As well as dignitaries from the County Education Committee and a fair sprinkling of local worthies, the rector of Thrush Green, the Reverend Octavius Fennel, was much in evidence. He opened the proceedings with a prayer, and also gave a short address, his text being: 'Suffer the little children to come unto me, and forbid them not; for of such is the Kingdom of God.'

A somewhat kindlier text, thought Alan, than the headmaster's original one.

Those present at this occasion were carefully listed, and one or two familiar names appeared, such as Lovelock and Harmer. Having found what he needed, Alan Lester returned the weighty volume to its resting place, and pondered on the most suitable festivities to promote on 20 September, 1992.

Meanwhile, Harold Shoosmith and Charles Henstock had been similarly engaged upon their researches, and were beginning to wonder about the best way to celebrate that other official opening, so far away under sunnier skies, at much the same time in 1892.

Both men had found Octavius's diary fascinating. The entries were brief, and one of the earliest was for 7 December, 1892. It read:

Received with joy letter from N. All well.

The diary was not kept daily, but very few weeks went by without some entry. Charles read it with particular sympathy. As he turned the pages, it became clear that his predecessor had been a man of outstanding kindliness and with a wide range of interests.

He obviously shared with so many Victorians the fascination of scientific discoveries. He mentioned meetings of the Lulling Scientific Society ('Lantern slides by courtesy of Oliver Lovelock, Esq.'). The Astronomer Royal had honoured them with a visit on his way to Somerset. He himself had felt obliged to speak out against some of the theories of Charles Darwin.

What came through most strongly was his steadfast belief in God and the teachings of the Anglican Church. Those theories of Charles Darwin's, about which he disapproved, were evidently contrary to his own religious beliefs and, no doubt, he looked upon them as heresy.

But the diary gave evidence not only of an upright man of God, but also of an endearing fellow who loved his neighbours, was compassionate and generous to the poor and sick, and was passionately fond of flowers, animals and the natural world about him.

Picked a dozen pyramid orchids by Lulling Woods. Took them with butter and eggs to poor old Biddy Bolton at Drovers' Arms. Lower limbs much afflicted with dropsy.

Entries mentioning Nathaniel came two or three times a year, each ending with 'see accounts'. It was plain that Octavius had financed this venture of Nathaniel's entirely from his own pocket.

By piecing together the material relating to Nathaniel in the diary, it was quite apparent to Charles and Harold that they now had a very good idea of the story.

Oliver Lovelock's useful article in 'Local Benefactors' on the subject of the Reverend Octavius Fennel was also very enlightening. Oliver obviously had great affection and respect for his clergyman friend, and also threw light on the relationship between Octavius and his protégé Nathaniel.

It appeared that the young missionary had been in his twenties when he embarked on his great adventure. There had been some preliminary correspondence with the Dr Maurice, already in Africa, mentioned in Nathaniel's first letter, and who was obviously about to welcome the young man on his arrival.

Oliver Lovelock's account gave something of Octavius's

background. His wealth came from the Lancashire cotton industry. The fact that earlier generations in his family had thrived at the expense of slave labour in the cotton fields of America seemed to weigh heavily upon the clergyman's conscience. Was this one of the reasons, wondered Charles and Harold, which prompted his compassion and generosity to his contemporaries?

As a young man he had travelled extensively, mainly in Europe, visiting various capitals rather in the manner of earlier travellers undertaking the Grand Tour. Russia in the days of the Tsar had much impressed the young man, and he evidently gave a lecture on the subject later in Lulling, according to Oliver Lovelock's biography.

After being ordained he spent some time in the poorer parts of London, taking great interest in the children, and in his early thirties he was given the living of Thrush Green, where he was to spend the rest of his life.

Charles Henstock's comment was typical. As a home-loving man himself, he told Harold that Octavius must have felt as if he had found a safe haven after so many trips abroad.

But Harold wondered if such a lively mind as Octavius's ever looked back upon his adventures with nostalgia. Would he ever have secret regrets for the life he had given up? On the other hand, Harold reminded himself, he, too, had travelled widely but had not regretted, for one instant, his decision to settle in the little world of Thrush Green.

No doubt Charles was right and Octavius was content with his lot. Certainly his diary gave proof of that.

There was a photocopying machine at the stationer's in Lulling High Street, and Harold used it to make copies of the relevant pages of 'Local Benefactors'.

On his way back, he called at the Lovelocks' house to return the leaflet and the torch to the ladies.

He was invited into the drawing-room, and sat among the clutter of occasional tables, armchairs, china cabinets, book cases and even a what-not, and told the three sisters how much he had appreciated their father's account of Octavius and his good works.

'My father had a great regard for him,' said Bertha. 'Of course, we hardly knew him, as we were in the nursery then. In fact, I doubt if Violet was born. If I remember rightly, Octavius died just before the 1914–18 war.'

'Quite right,' said Harold.

'He brought Father a charming little paperknife from St Petersburg. It is still on the desk in his study.'

'And he gave us a Russian egg,' recalled Ada. 'I wonder what happened to it?'

'I think I saw it in the loft,' Harold told them, 'with other toys.'

'One day,' said Bertha, 'we must get someone to clear out that loft for us, and dispose of the contents.'

She gazed speculatively at Harold. He saw again, in his mind's eye, the stack of iron bedsteads, the heavy trunks crammed with the detritus of years, the decrepit chairs, the hip baths, the towel rails and the floor sprinkled with mouse droppings.

'I really must be off,' he said rising. 'Thank you again for your help. Your father's notes have been invaluable.'

Violet escorted him to the front door.

'What a nice man!' she remarked to her sisters when she returned. 'And he has put a new battery in the torch, too.'

'We may as well keep it downstairs,' said Ada. 'There's no point in having a new battery in a torch which is going to be kept in the loft.'

'It would be a wicked waste,' agreed Bertha. 'Put it in the hall, Violet dear; it will save us switching on the electric light.'

The diary was probably of greater interest to Charles than to Harold, for the good rector was intrigued with the view of Thrush Green and Lulling seen through the eyes of a man doing the same work a century earlier in much the same surroundings.

He was as much impressed as Harold with the portrait of the man which emerged. He took a lively interest in his natural surroundings, his parishioners, and also in wider issues such as the conditions of the workers in industry, the might of the British Empire and the uneasy state of Europe.

Charles was interested to see his predecessor's comments on new scientific discoveries, but noted, too, how steadfastly he set his face against anything which, in his opinion, threatened the teachings of the Church. He spoke scathingly of spiritualism, and deplored the use of such toys as ouija boards, and the gatherings of people at seances, in attempts to get into touch with other worlds.

Across the years he spoke to Charles as a friendly, highly intelligent and thoughtful man. He possessed an intellect, Charles recognized humbly, far in advance of his own. But one thing they shared in common. They did indeed love their God.

It was Nathaniel's letters which gave Harold the most acute joy. Just to touch those frail pieces of paper, and to know that Nathaniel's hand had rested where his now lay, gave him a feeling of kinship and exquisite pleasure.

The diary had given only the briefest hint, now and again, of the strong bond between the two men: a father-and-son relationship as well as true friendship, for Octavius was some twenty years older than Nathaniel, and was also in a position to help the younger man, not only with his wisdom and advice, but also with regular and generous donations, as the accounts showed.

Occasionally, there had been a wistful and fatherly comment in the diary.

Only God can understand my grief at N.'s determination not to take Holy Orders. But N. is a fine young man, and God guides him as He does me. We are in His hands.

Nathaniel's letters threw more light on this vexed question. To Harold's disappointment, he soon discovered that a great many of the letters were missing. There were references to earlier matters, and it was clear, from the carefully dated relics, that only about a third of the letters were remaining.

From these, however, it was plain that Nathaniel grieved as sorely as his benefactor about his inability to enter the Anglican Church.

Your unfailing goodness to me [he wrote in 1895] *is my constant support and inspiration. It makes my seeming opposition to your wishes, in the matter of taking Holy Orders, doubly painful to me, and I should be a happier man if my conscience would allow me to follow your dictates. As it is, I know that you understand my feelings, and will not allow this basic difference to injure the friendship we share under God's blessing.*

There was no mention of Nathaniel's marriage, either, in the remaining letter nor, strangely enough, in Octavius's diary, but later letters mentioned his dead wife, and the little daughter whom he proposed to send to friends in England for her education.

As a murky January drew to its close, Harold and Charles

realized that there would be very little more to be discovered about the long-dead friends.

All that remained now, they agreed, was to choose a fitting tribute to honour two fine men of Thrush Green.

6. Hard Weather

February came in with the same dismal clammy weather which had held sway throughout January. But after the first week, the weathervanes spun round to the north-east, and a vicious wind tossed the bare branches of the chestnut trees on Thrush Green.

It was during this bleak spell that Winnie Bailey was admitted to hospital, for the various tests had shown that it was, as suspected, gall bladder trouble, and surgery would, after all, be needed.

Speculation on the outcome of the operation was rife at The Two Pheasants.

Albert Piggott told Percy Hodge that, in his opinion, no one was ever the same again.

'My old uncle what was gamekeeper up Nidden was on slops for the rest of his life. Rice pudden, mashed potato, drop of broth – that was all he could take.'

Percy was unimpressed. 'My Gladys,' he replied, naming his present wife, 'says it don't make a mite of difference having your gall bladder out. Some bits of us are real useless. Look at my appendix, for instance.'

But nobody appeared to be interested in Percy's appendix, which perhaps was just as well because it had been removed years earlier.

Mr Jones, who rather fancied himself as a medical man, a

sort of hedge-doctor, told the assembled company that you could blast gallstones into dust with a few shots of laser rays, but you had to be careful that they didn't damage the red corpuscles.

Blinded with such sophisticated knowledge, the company dropped the subject of gall bladders and their treatment, but all agreed that Mrs Bailey 'would have to watch it' when she came out of hospital.

'If she ever does,' said Albert lugubriously. He liked to have the last word.

News of Winnie had reached, via Isobel Shoosmith, the two retired schoolteachers at Barton-on-Sea.

Loving messages had been despatched to St Richard's, and Interflora had been directed to send a flower arrangement to their old friend.

'I told them to send a *small* one,' Dorothy told Agnes. 'The right size for a bedside locker but smelling particularly sweet. Freesias, say, or carnations. I must say that the girl who replied seemed to understand what was wanted.'

'I'm sure she knows all about flowers for hospitals,' Agnes assured her.

'Well, I don't know about that! When I did my leg I had great towering bouquets of irises and gladioli, I remember, and the nurses were quite cross. They would keep falling over. The vases, I mean, not the nurses.'

Later that day Dorothy had a bright idea. 'Do you think Winnie would like a week or so here when she is convalescent? We could easily put her up, and the air here is so particularly good. It might be just the thing to pull her round.'

Agnes was delighted with the idea, and the evening was spent in happy anticipation of entertaining an invalid in the good air of Barton-on-Sea whenever she felt ready to accept their invitation.

But just as Agnes's euphoria was at its height, a chance remark of Dorothy's as they made their way to bed caused it to plummet.

'By the way, I wrote a little note to Alan Lester yesterday, to see if I could be of any help in those centenary celebrations Isobel mentioned.'

Agnes said nothing, but once in bed her fears flocked round her like a plague of bats.

What might come of this? Why must dear Dorothy, for the best of reasons, of course, feel obliged to *meddle*!

Ella Bembridge struggled against an icy wind to pay a brief visit to Dotty Harmer's cottage.

The sky above Lulling Woods was ominous, the clouds low and a menacing grey. If that doesn't mean snow, Ella told herself, I'm a Dutchman.

She found Dotty, as before, at her kitchen table surrounded by papers.

'My word,' said Ella, 'you look as though you're halfway through that book of yours.'

'I don't know about that,' replied Dotty, thrusting her pen through her scanty hair. 'I'm getting rather tired of literary work.'

'Why? What's put you off?'

'I showed my manuscript to Harold, and he said that it wouldn't make one chapter, let alone a whole book, and he couldn't see any publisher taking it on. I said to him: "What about all those reviews talking about 'this slim volume' and 'a charming monograph of a much-loved father' and all that sort of thing?" But he still says it's not long enough.'

'So what will you do? Scrap it?'

'*Scrap it?*' squeaked Dotty indignantly. 'After all my hard work? Of course I shan't scrap it!'

'Well, it seems a bit pointless to carry on,' said Ella. 'Can't you pad it out somehow?'

'I do not propose to lower my standards for the sake of *length*,' said Dotty loftily, 'but I have had another idea. I have asked a number of old boys of the grammar school to write down their memories of my father, and I intend to incorporate them.'

'A splendid notion,' said Ella.

Dotty shuffled the papers before her with a claw-like hand. She looked perplexed.

'The only thing is that they all seem to dwell on Father's disciplinary side, and it makes him appear in rather a harsh light. I hoped they would discuss his fine mind, his interest in astronomy and photography. After all, he founded several scientific clubs at the school, and was most generous with gifts to the science side. I remember him handing over his own microscope and an auxanometer.'

'And what's that?'

'Well, dear, I rather forget, but I've an idea it measures the growth of plants. Father was a great botanist as well as everything else. I must say, I am rather disgusted with these old boys' narrow views.'

'Then I shouldn't use them,' said Ella stoutly. 'Just finish your notes and publish them privately.'

Dotty looked more cheerful at this gleam of hope for her cherished work. 'I am sure you are right, Ella. And now let me make you a drink. Some of my lime-flower tisane, or a cup of Nescafé?'

'I think Nescafé,' said Ella, who had tried Dotty's concoctions too often for comfort.

A quarter of an hour later she left Dotty sorting out her papers, and stepped out into the bleak world. A few flakes of snow were fluttering down, and by the time she emerged from the field path on to Thrush Green, a whirling mass of snowflakes gave promise of a white world before morning.

From her hospital bed Winnie watched the snowstorm spreading a carpet of white and shaking the trees in the grounds. It made a strange contrast with the over-heated room, heavy with the mingled scent of flowers, floor polish and disinfectant.

On her locker stood the bouquet from Dorothy and Agnes, and another from Jenny. More flowers lined the windowsills and a side table, and Winnie thought how lucky she was to have so many loving friends.

Among other things on the locker top stood a glass screw-top jar containing a number of dark objects ranging in size from walnuts to peppercorns. Winnie had screened this from her own gaze by propping up a large 'get-well' card in front of it, for it was a gruesome reminder of Mr Philip Paterson's (St Thomas's) successful surgery a few days earlier, and Winnie felt she could not face its presence much longer.

Winnie's first impulse had been to beg her nurse to throw the lot in the hospital dustbin, but when several colleagues burst in to look at the jar with awe and delight, she felt unequal to the effort. When the surgeon visited her that evening she hoped that he would remove the revolting jar, but he was even more delighted than the nurses at the result of his skills.

'Do you think,' said Winnie faintly, 'that they could be thrown away now that I've seen them?'

Mr Paterson clutched the jar to him, as a mother might clutch her baby. 'But surely you want to take them home?'

The very thought sent a wave of nausea through poor Winnie, but as a doctor's wife she did her duty. 'I think you did a wonderful job,' she said, 'and I shall always be grateful. But I cannot have those ghastly things here any longer.'

Mr Paterson appeared astounded. 'Well,' he said, looking deeply hurt, 'I'll leave them where they were on the locker, in case you change your mind, and you can have a look later. After supper, say. I believe you are having a little fish soup tonight.'

He gave his usual comforting smile and departed.

Really a charming fellow, thought Winnie, and so conscientious with his night and morning visits.

Nevertheless, she resolved to get one of the nurses to dispose of the jar, and if she and the other girls complained of such ruthlessness it was just too bad.

As for Philip Paterson, he would have to endure the loss of his handiwork with all the fortitude of a true St Thomas's man.

The snowstorm raged for over twenty-four hours, leaving the Cotswolds in a white shroud. The dry-stone walls surrounding the fields had disappeared beneath drifts, leaving vast expanses of unbroken snow, reminiscent of the steppes of Russia or the awesome wastes of Antarctica. The steep roofs were covered, and all the stone house walls which faced north and east were plastered with frozen snow. When the sun appeared, low on the horizon for about three hours of the day, it did little to mitigate the intensity of the cold.

In Lulling the main road was soon cleared, and those leading south to the coast and north to the Midlands had first attention. But Thrush Green and the lanes leading from it remained snow-covered for almost a week, and people were obliged to stay indoors until the thaw arrived.

This was no hardship for Winnie Bailey, now in her own home and relishing the comfort of her own bed and the ministrations of Jenny and John Lovell. She was making a steady recovery from surgery, and could potter about the house and help Jenny with a little cooking and cleaning, but she was surprised, and secretly ashamed, at the weakness which engulfed her every now and again, and realized that even if the weather had been kindly she could not have gone very far outdoors.

It was at times like these, she thought, that the telephone really came into its own. Friends rang to enquire about her progress;

and among the enquiries was a welcome call from Dorothy Watson inviting her to stay at Barton when the weather allowed, and she felt strong enough to face the journey.

Gazing at her snow-filled garden through the window, at the sagging branches of the bare plum tree and the ancient cypress which Donald had planted, she felt a wild longing to see and smell the sea again.

'There is nothing I should enjoy more,' she told Dorothy. 'The very thought of it is wonderfully cheering. I shall look forward to it eagerly.'

'Then I shall get in touch again,' promised Dorothy, 'as soon as it's possible to travel.'

After a little more exchange of news Dorothy put down the telephone.

'She would like to come,' she told Agnes, who had just emerged from the bathroom with her newly washed hair tied up in a towelling turban.

'Perfect!' said Agnes.

And when Jenny brought Winnie's supper to her that evening she stood and surveyed her with considerable satisfaction.

'You look a lot stronger,' she told her. 'Turned the corner, as they say. What's done it, do you think?'

'The thought of seeing the sea again,' replied Winnie. 'And, of course, good friends.'

The number of children at Thrush Green school was almost halved during the worst of the snowy weather.

For two days the school bus was closeted in its garage, and the pupils from outlying parts were joyful prisoners in their homes. There were quite a few children who lived closer to the green, but were equally imprisoned by high drifts between their homes and the school.

Added to this was a spate of winter coughs and colds which

kept children indoors, and John Lovell busy on his rounds. His usual car was sealed in the garage for three days before he and helpers could dig it out, but his brother-in-law, the architect Edward Young, lent him his Land Rover during the worst of the weather, so that the patients who needed attention urgently could be visited.

As soon as it was possible to get about again, Charles Henstock paid a visit to Harold Shoosmith.

'It was about fixing a date for our celebration,' began Charles. 'Alan Lester tells me that his school was opened formally in August a hundred years ago.'

'That's rather early for us to think of combining our festivities, if that's what you had in mind.'

'I agree,' said the rector, 'but the *official* opening of the school, he has discovered, was on 20 September of that year, and that makes things seem easier.'

'Is he agreeable to sharing festivities?'

'Indeed he is! And so am I, but how do you feel? I know you want to give full honours to Nathaniel and Octavius. Would you mind if we combined?'

'Not at all,' said Harold sturdily. 'In many ways it will make everything better. After all, we are all part of Thrush Green, young and old, alive and dead. I'm all in favour of one great day we can share.'

'Well, I must admit that I am relieved,' confessed Charles. 'You've worked so hard at your researches into the history of our two friends that I didn't want your efforts to be overshadowed by the school's celebration.'

'I'll have a word with Lester if you like,' said Harold. 'What would be best, do you think?'

'Late September seems the obvious choice, doesn't it? The new term will have begun, and the weather should be fine for outdoor affairs.'

And so it was left.

The next day Isobel invited Alan and his wife to have a drink and discuss the matter, but their two little girls were among Thrush Green's juvenile patients, and the invitation was reversed, so that the invalids need not be left alone.

Margaret Lester greeted them affectionately. The little girls had left their beds and, clad in nightgowns, called their greetings over the landing handrail.

'Now get back quickly,' ordered their mother, 'or those coughs will start again, and you don't want any more of Dr Lovell's cough mixture, do you?'

'Is it as bad as that?' queried Harold, as the two children vanished.

'I believe so. Ruth Lovell told me that John never dreams of taking his own cough mixture. But to give him his due, the stuff does seem to work.'

It was very snug in the school house sitting-room. The log fire crackled, the red-shaded lamps gave a warm glow, and the drinks gave an inner one.

The matter of a date for a joint celebration was soon under discussion, both men being very careful to respect the other's wishes.

'The only rough plan I've made so far,' said Alan, 'is to have the minimum of activities outside. I've had too many occasions washed out during my teaching days, and now I settle for something indoors.'

'Very wise,' said Harold. 'I'm sure our own ideas will match that. In any case, I think a celebratory memorial service in the church is in the rector's mind, and I'm sure that will be the chief part. After all, both men were churchmen first and foremost.'

'Miss Robinson had the bright idea of a day in the school as it might have been a hundred years ago. We've a pretty good idea of the timetable, and the children will enjoy dressing up. We could even have the cane in evidence!'

'I wonder if it was used much,' mused Isobel.

'According to the first log book,' Alan told her, 'it was kept pretty busy on one or two of the older boys who would far rather have been out in the fields.'

'No doubt the farmers could do with them,' commented Harold. 'And a few extra coppers would be welcome in any farm labourer's home, from all I can gather. Octavius's diary gives a glimpse of rural hard times. Some of those fellows must literally have been worked to an early death, as one or two records show.'

Alan began to turn over the leaves of a calendar. 'Now, I think you said that the mission station was opened on 1 October. That's a Thursday. It would fit in with school affairs very well.'

Harold felt greatly pleased. He had secretly hoped that the exact date of Nathaniel's mission-opening would be kept, but having agreed to co-operate with the school's centenary he had been quite prepared to give way.

'It would give me great pleasure,' he told Alan, and despite the formality of the words, it was apparent to all present that he felt enormously grateful.

'We'll be present at the service, of course, as a school, I mean,' went on Alan, 'and I shall make a point of telling the children all I can about the lives of the two men. I just wonder, though, if we could have a real Thrush Green beano at that time, on the green itself.'

'We'll think about it,' said Harold. 'As you say, the chief part of the celebrations will be under cover, but we ought to be able to risk at least an hour or two for a general jollification outside.'

The date having been provisionally fixed, the talk grew more general.

'I must say there seems to be a lot of interest in these affairs,' said Alan. 'Our Parent–Teacher Association wants to take part. They'll be very useful in the dressing-up side of my project.'

'And someone said that they thought we ought to try to raise some money to buy something – a tree, perhaps,' said Margaret.

'No doubt Charles will put a note about it in the parish magazine and get ideas from people,' said Isobel.

'By the way,' said Alan, 'I had a letter from Dorothy Watson offering to help with any school festivities.'

'Oh!' said Isobel and Harold at the same time, and with an identical tone of apprehension.

'Very kind,' said Alan firmly, 'but I shall turn down the offer as politely as I can.'

Relief was apparent on his guests' faces, but no further comment was made, and before long the party broke up.

Some days later Dorothy Watson read out a letter to Agnes as they sat at breakfast in Barton-on-Sea.

'Just listen to this. From Alan Lester!'

Agnes felt a little shiver of fear. Was he cross? She put down her egg spoon and listened obediently.

Dorothy cleared her throat, just as she used to do before addressing Thrush Green school at morning assembly.

Dear Miss Watson,
Your kind offer of help in connection with our proposed activities is very much appreciated.

As you may imagine, at this early stage we are still weighing up various possibilities, but I am quite positive about keeping things as simple as we can.

I look forward to letting you know our plans as soon as

they are made, and of course you and Miss Fogerty will be among our most honoured guests.

Dorothy beamed across the table at her friend. Agnes felt relief flooding her.

'A very nice letter,' she ventured.

'And so sensible to keep things simple,' agreed Dorothy. 'I always felt that we had left the school in safe hands.'

Agnes took up her egg spoon again. She could not help but recall the doubts her friend had expressed vigorously about the headmaster who had been appointed in her place. Was he *competent*? Was he *understanding*? Was it *wise* of him to live at a distance, as he certainly did when he first took up the post? And above all, would he carry on the methods of his predecessor which had been so much valued by pupils, staff and parents alike?

Agnes had done her best to counter her headmistress's fears during those last hectic weeks of their teaching days, and had endured many private sufferings.

But now, sitting at the breakfast table, with Alan Lester's letter lying between them, was not the moment to remind her friend of those earlier misgivings.

Dorothy had gradually come to accept the fact that her school was safe in Alan Lester's hands. What was more, she began to feel considerable respect for the way he was coping.

And now he had written most kindly, appreciating her offer of advice and help, and promising to keep them informed. Better still was the thought of visiting Thrush Green school again, 'as honoured guests', and taking part in its festivities.

'I always liked that man,' said Dorothy, reaching for the toast.

'Me too,' echoed Agnes. 'He always struck me as *wise*.'

7. COMINGS AND GOINGS

As so often happens when a perfectly simple project is planned, complications and difficulties arose.

The rector had put a short message in the parish magazine announcing the proposed date and the fact that it seemed appropriate for the two celebrations to combine.

The poor man at once received a number of notes and telephone calls pointing out that they – the writers and ringers – would be:

a) away from home
b) attending a much more important function in London or the county town
c) were expecting confinements, visits from relatives recuperating from illness, or were proposing to enter hospital at the time stated.

Harold Shoosmith told him to 'let them get on with it'. But he, too, had his critics, and none more vociferous than Mrs Gibbons who lived far too near him for comfort.

The Gibbons were newcomers to Thrush Green and had embraced village life with a fervour unknown to the local population. They were soon enrolled as chairmen, secretaries, treasurers, and so on, of almost all the village activities, much to the relief and amusement of their lazier neighbours.

As Mr Gibbons was still working in some unspecified but highly important business in London, it was Mrs Gibbons who was more in evidence, although she was always keen to stress the support she had from her husband who, she hinted darkly, wielded power over a great many influential people in government circles.

Harold Shoosmith had secretly dubbed him 'Gauleiter Gibbons'; certainly when he did take charge of any village meeting he was as dictatorial as his spouse, and Harold always had the feeling that a banner should be waving behind him, and that the assembled company should rise, chanting, to its feet when the leader appeared.

Harold was unfortunate enough to encounter Mrs Gibbons one morning, as he was coming back from the postbox.

'Ah! Just the man I wanted to see!' she carolled.

Harold's heart sank.

'I believe you started this ballyhoo about the great Nathaniel,' she continued, with dreadful facetiousness.

Harold's heart ascended again. No one, and certainly not Mrs Gibbons, was going to denigrate Nathaniel in his presence.

'Of course, any jollifications should be put in charge of the Thrush Green entertainments committee, of which I am chairman.'

'I know,' said Harold.

'And as for the school's celebration, that of course should be a matter for discussion between the headmaster and the Parent–Teacher Association, of which again, I am the chairman.'

'I know,' repeated Harold.

'I've a mind to call on Alan Lester now, while I'm here,' said the lady sharply.

'He's just gone off to Cornwall,' Harold told her, with considerable satisfaction. 'School ended last week.'

'I'm quite aware of that,' snapped Mrs Gibbons.

'In any case,' Harold pointed out, 'things have hardly begun to move yet. All that has happened is plainly laid out in this month's parish magazine. So far, we've simply planned a date convenient to everyone—'

'How do you know it's convenient to *everyone*?' cried Mrs Gibbons, flushing pink.

'And announced the Sunday chosen for the combined service,' continued Harold equably. 'Now if you will excuse me, I must hurry home. I am expecting a telephone call.'

No doubt the Gauleiter would hear all about this encounter when he arrived home from running the nation, thought Harold. Poor devil!

The ladies of Thrush Green had decked St Andrew's church for Easter, and its Victorian plainness was adorned with daffodils and narcissi on every windowsill, little bunches of violets and primroses arranged by the children at the foot of the font, and some magnificent hot-house lilies on the altar.

The Reverend Charles Henstock and the choir made their entry by the west door that morning, and proceeded down the aisle to the cheerful strains of 'Christ is Risen', sung with great gusto by all present.

Winnie Bailey, standing in her usual place, thought what a joyful celebration Easter was. There were some lovely hymns, the spring flowers were doubly beautiful after the darkness of winter, and the time of the year was full of hope.

The sun, streaming through the east and south windows, threw shafts of coloured light upon the altar and the chancel floor. No one could truthfully say that the stained glass of St Andrew's had much to commend it, but in the general rejoicing of Easter it added to the church's ambience.

Charles would be busy today, thought Winnie, settling back to listen to the first lesson. This morning's service had been arranged for ten o'clock, enabling the rector to hurry back to St John's for Matins at eleven fifteen, in Lulling. Cold lunch for most of us today, she thought, rising for the next hymn.

The movement brought a wave of dizziness, and she was obliged to hold on to the pew until it passed. Please don't let me fall down in front of everyone, she prayed fervently! A twinge of the old pain made her grit her teeth, but within a minute or two she felt better again.

She started to sing with the rest of the congregation. Words by S. Baring-Gould, she noticed. Donald had had a great regard for the Reverend S. Baring-Gould.

> *On the Resurrection morning*
> *Soul and body meet again;*
> *No more sorrow, no more weeping,*
> *No more pain.*

Perhaps that's a good omen, Winnie told herself. I must cross my fingers!

But wasn't that rather inappropriate – pagan, even; omens

and crossed fingers in the middle of a Church of England festival? Amused at her thoughts, the pain gone, Winnie raised her voice in praise.

Not long after this, when Thrush Green school was open again, a meeting for all interested was held to go through the suggestions put forward for the two celebrations.

The rector took the chair, and there were more people present than he had expected. Mrs Gibbons was in the front row, seated on one of the children's chairs, for the meeting was being held in the school.

One good thing about the venue, Harold Shoosmith thought to himself, was the fact that the school chairs were so ill-suited to the adult form that the business under discussion got done pretty smartly.

He himself had taken up a strategic and more comfortable position on one of the desk tops, which gave him more room for his long legs. Alan Lester, he noticed, had done the same, having relinquished his headmaster's wooden armchair to the rector on this occasion.

The first proposal to be put was that of combining the two celebrations – the centenary of the school in which they sat, and the centenary of the opening of Nathaniel's mission.

There was surprisingly little discussion on this point. Even Mrs Gibbons, who usually argued at public meetings as a matter of course, seemed to think that a joint celebration had much to commend it.

'Although,' she remarked in her ringing voice, 'with all due respect to our chairman, one wonders if these celebrations may not turn out to be rather too *Anglican*. We must keep in mind that there are a great many people who belong to other denominations. We don't want them to feel excluded.'

'I can assure you,' replied Charles Henstock patiently, 'that all will be invited. Certainly, I myself have approached the other church ministers in the area, and they are enthusiastic in coming to the church service here at St Andrew's, as well as the general celebrations.'

'Anyway,' boomed Ella Bembridge from the back of the room, 'it's a Church of England school, and dear old Nathaniel was an out-and-out Church of England chap, even if he didn't actually take Holy Orders, so what's wrong with bearing that in mind?'

There were general noises of agreement. The proposal to combine was put and carried overwhelmingly.

The rector gave plans and date for the church celebration, and Alan Lester outlined his idea for a Victorian day at the school. There was great enthusiasm for the latter, and several people offered articles of apparel, books and bric-à-brac which had belonged to Victorian forebears.

Alan Lester was plainly delighted at this response and, striking while the iron was hot, said that he would be looking for volunteers nearer the time to help with the dressing of the children and general assistance.

There was a buzz of offers and conversation became general. The rector, quite accustomed to this sort of thing at village meetings, waited indulgently for the gossip to die down before coming to the chief problem.

'Now we are all agreed on the general form of our festivities,' he began, 'which as I'm sure you have noticed will take place under cover. But it has been suggested that we might risk just one outside event.'

'In October?' said one.

'Best be a Saturday then,' said another.

'That's right. It'll be dark around six.'

'Weather's tricky then.'

Thus spoke the more pessimistic of those present, but there were several more optimistic voices raised.

'What about a tea party? Trestle tables and all that, like after the war?'

'Might be warm enough. Have to wear a coat, though, in October.'

'I reckon a tug-of-war would fit the bill.'

'They had a dance up Nidden one year, out in the open, with fairy lights and that in the trees.'

'But the wind got up, remember? Couldn't hear the band. That was one autumn, as I recollect.'

The rector, who had been noting down suggestions, waited, pen poised, for the tumult to subside.

When at last it did, there was a scuffling at the back and Gladys Hodge, the wife of Percy the local farmer, spoke up. She was much respected in the community, and the general opinion was that Percy, who had lost two wives and been turned down by various other ladies, suitable and unsuitable, had done very well for himself in this recent marriage.

Gladys had raised one hand to command the chairman's attention, and was nudging a pink-faced Percy with the other.

'My husband,' said Gladys, 'has a suggestion.'

Percy, much flustered, was pushed to his feet.

'Well,' he began, 'I know all about it being October and maybe cold or windy or too dark too soon, and all that caper, but what about 5 November?'

'What about it?' said one.

'That's Guy Fawkes, soppy,' said another.

'We're talking about 1 October, Perce.'

'I know, I know!' cried Percy doggedly, 'but what I'm saying is, we know everyone comes to Bonfire Night and we all has a rattling good time, even if it is dark, and the fire keeps us warm if it's cold, and the kids love it as much as us old 'uns, and I'll be pleased to give the potatoes to bake in the ashes, for this occasion, just like I always do for Guy Fawkes.'

At this he sat down abruptly on to his uncomfortable chair, and there was a murmur of general approval.

Mrs Gibbons was heard to say that *two* Bonfire Nights were surely too much.

'Can't have *too much* of a good thing,' said Ella loudly, 'and I think it's a grand idea.'

It certainly seemed to please those present, and the rector put Percy's proposal to the meeting. All hands, it seemed, were raised, and the rector thanked Percy for his inspired suggestion, and for the generous offer of baked potatoes which, as was customary, would be cooked by the boy scouts, if that would be all right with the scoutmaster.

He, unfortunately, was not present to clinch the matter.

'Gone to his auntie's funeral.'

'Fell off a ladder and bust his collarbone.'

'Goes to Morris dancing every Wednesday.'

These were a few of the explanations given for the scout-master's absence. As a matter of fact, he had completely for-gotten about the meeting, and was lime-washing his henhouse ready for the summer.

The rector promised to get in touch with him, thanked everyone present, and the meeting drew to a close.

'Come and have a drink,' said Harold to Charles as the gathering broke up.

'I should like that,' said Charles. 'I find meetings rather tiring, I must say.'

'You're a first-class chairman,' Harold told him as they walked next door to the Shoosmiths' house.

'Oh, no, indeed!' protested Charles. 'I fear I let people talk too much.'

'That's why I say you are a first-class chairman,' repeated

Harold. 'And just right for Thrush Green. Everyone goes home happy. In your place I should have got through the business in half the time, and made a host of enemies.'

He pushed open the front door, and Isobel was there to welcome them.

In the same week it was Isobel who drove Winnie Bailey down to Barton-on-Sea to spend a few days with her old friends Dorothy and Agnes.

Dorothy had offered to fetch Winnie in her Metro, but Isobel pointed out that it would be simpler if she could bring their visitor, as she, too, would like to have a few breaths of sea air.

Privately, she felt that Winnie would have a more comfortable and peaceful journey in her Audi, for she herself seldom spoke when she was at the wheel, and she knew that Dorothy kept up a loud monologue, accompanied by waving hands, which could tire and alarm a nervous passenger.

Agnes had prepared a delicious lunch of chicken and ham with pineapple, in a creamy sauce, which was followed by sherry trifle. Replete, the ladies sat in the sunny sitting-room with their coffee, and exchanged news.

Tim, the cat, sat purring on Winnie's knee, and Isobel remembered the trouble his advent had caused between the two old friends. Dorothy had set her face against Agnes's adoption of the stray at first, but Agnes had been so seriously upset that the animal had been accepted into the household, and now, as is the way with cats, quite obviously ruled the roost.

Observing the two friends, looking so relaxed and happy, Isobel recalled another crisis in their lives when Dorothy had become greatly attached to a Barton neighbour. Agnes had confided in Isobel that she was afraid that Dorothy was pursuing this attractive widower with the hope of matrimony. It had been an unhappy time for poor Agnes, envisaging her own search for a new abode should her friend's hopes material-ize and the bungalow they shared become a love-nest for the mature pair.

Fortunately, Teddy had fallen for the charms of another local lady, and it was apparent, from the cheerful way Dorothy spoke about them, that her romantic notions had vanished. Dear me, thought Isobel, what a nuisance love can be!

The news from Thrush Green was eagerly welcomed, and the plans for the school's Victorian day much praised.

'As a matter of fact,' asserted Dorothy, 'I had much the same idea in mind when I offered any help I could give to Alan Lester. We had a charming letter from him,' she added.

'Well, I hope you will stay with us for the celebrations,' said Isobel. 'And we'll make sure that you see all your old friends. It's going to be a great event.'

They all took a turn by the sea in the afternoon, relishing the blue skies and blue sea, and the promise of summer ahead.

Isobel set off after tea so that she could make her journey back in the light.

The three friends waved her off, and Isobel felt sure that Winnie was in safe hands.

It was a beautiful drive back: first through the New Forest, hazy with the new green leaves of spring, then through the rolling Hampshire countryside as she went north.

The crops were beginning to spring, clothing the fields with tender green. Celandines starred the banks in the sunshine of late afternoon, and small birds darted across the road, trailing dried grass or the odd feather, as they busied themselves with their nests. The hawthorn hedges were showing their first red shoots, and soon the copses on either side of the road would be misty with bluebells.

April, thought Isobel, had its charms, and also its hazards. The clear sky above her might well presage a frost tonight. Her favourite month was May when blackthorn blossom made snowy drifts in the hedgerows, and wild cherry blossom lit the woods.

She looked forward to the garden blossom too: the white cherry hanging its snowy fringe along the branches, the plum trees scattering their pale confetti, and later the rosy knots of apple buds on the trees planted in their garden by some long-dead owner.

As she drove, the look of the countryside changed gradually. The flint and brick cottages with their thatched or tiled roofs began to give way to the stone-built buildings of the Cotswolds, their steep gables silhouetted against the now-darkening sky.

The lights were beginning to glow from windows at Thrush Green when Isobel ended her journey.

She shivered as she stepped from the car. The Cotswold air was sharper than that at Barton-on-Sea, and frost might well touch them here tonight. She noticed a plume of smoke rising from the chimney of her home, and felt a surge of pleasure at the thought of an evening by the fire.

Perhaps, after all, April was a perfect month. It combined the outdoor joys of spring and the equally enjoyable pleasure of the domestic fireside. Her favourite month was still May, she told herself, but meanwhile she would be very content to take all that April offered.

Later that evening, stretched out by the welcome fire, their feet on footstools, Harold and Isobel exchanged the news of the day.

'And to see the sea again was a bonus,' added Isobel when she had described the old friends' welcome, and Winnie's pleasure at seeing them again. 'I wish we were nearer. Nothing can beat a walk on the sands, or on a cliff top.'

'My walk,' said Harold, 'was much less exciting. Just along Lulling High Street to get some half-inch screws. Still, I did bump into the Lovelock sisters.'

'And what were they doing?'

'Going into The Fuchsia Bush for their lunch, I gather. We had quite a gossip. They were very good about lending me that pamphlet of their father's.'

He began to look rather uneasy, and cleared his throat before speaking again.

'I thought – er – I wondered if it might be nice to invite them up for tea one day.'

'Nice for whom?'

'Oh, come on, darling! Don't be awkward. I just felt we should do something about them as they helped me with that essay abut Octavius.'

Isobel smiled forgivingly. 'They can come, but you know how I feel about those dreadful old harpies. We shall have to hide all the bits of silver from their beady eyes.'

'Oh, and I saw Charles. He and Dimity are going to a concert at the Barbican.'

'Good heavens! How dashing of them!'

'Robert Wilberforce has invited them. Evidently he's down in London for a day or two on business.'

'I hope Charles isn't thinking of driving. Parking's bad enough in Lulling, let alone London.'

'No. They're going up by train, he said, and Robert is meeting them at Paddington. I'm so glad for them. They get away so seldom. They seem really excited.'

'Well,' said Isobel, yawning. 'I think it's bedtime. It's been a long day, and I've a lot to do tomorrow.'

'Don't forget to ring the Lovelocks,' Harold reminded her.

'I'm not likely to forget that,' Isobel told him tartly.

8. Plans Go Ahead

As the summer term progressed, preparations for Thrush Green school's centenary celebrations started to take shape.

Few preparations were necessary for the school's part in the church service, or in the general joint celebrations, in which it would participate with even greater fervour, one suspected, but the Victorian day at the school needed more particular care.

Alan Lester called upon the Parent–Teacher Association to co-ordinate the plans. It was as well, he thought, to get the formidable Mrs Gibbons on his side without more ado, and in any case it was only right and proper that they should take an active part.

Many of the parents were old pupils. Some grandparents were, too, and although of course, there was no one alive who could remember the school as it was in 1892, there were a number who had heard their own parents and grandparents talking of their schooldays. This sense of continuity in a small community touched Alan Lester deeply.

He was delighted at the general enthusiasm for the idea of a Victorian schoolday when he spoke to the assembled company one evening.

Mrs Gibbons, in the chair, occasionally raised a query, but he felt it was more as a way of reminding them all that she was in charge, rather than from a genuine desire to alter the arrangements.

'The daily timetable for that period,' Alan told the gathering, 'is clearly set out in the first log book, and I have left it open on the desk, in front of Mrs Gibbons, so that you can have a look at it later.'

Mrs Gibbons tapped the stout volume in a proprietorial manner. 'Only *three* at a time,' she said. 'Otherwise it will be difficult to study it. And *after* these proceedings, of course.'

'Of course,' agreed Alan, giving her the smile which disarmed even such dragons as the present chairman.

'The biggest problem,' he went on, 'is finding the right furniture of the time. There were long desks for six pupils then, and of course most of them vanished long ago. I have discovered a couple at Nidden school which closed some time ago, and I think we can borrow them.'

'There's one in my dad's garage,' said one mother. 'He bought it off of the chap as was at the sale years ago.'

'And the chapel's got a couple in the back kitchen,' called another. 'They keeps the tea urns and china and that on 'em.'

'They did have one up the cricket pavilion,' said a third, 'but some kids got in and scandalized it one night. Daubed paint on it. Might be all right if you could get the paint off of it.'

'This is marvellous news,' exclaimed Alan, turning the smile on Mrs Gibbons, who had begun to tap her pencil vigorously on his desk to draw attention to the fact that questions were not being addressed to the chair.

One would have imagined, thought Alan, still smiling, that any chairman in Thrush Green, or any other village community for that matter, would be quite resigned to the general conversation which took over proceedings every now and again.

'I must say, *through the chair*,' he said, 'how grateful I am for these suggestions. I shall follow them up, and if anyone has any news of other contemporary school fittings I should be delighted to hear about them. If not, we might get some made.'

Mrs Gibbons smiled graciously and the pencil stopped tapping. 'Now, about clothes,' she said briskly. 'Mr Lester has pictures of the sort of thing the children would have worn then. The Misses Lovelock have kindly lent some old family photos. They are on the wall there. You might like to study them when you come, *three at a time*, to see the log book.'

'The urn's bubbling,' said someone. 'Shall I make the coffee?'

A look of exasperation passed over the chairman's face, but she spoke patiently. 'Very well. Better perhaps to have our refreshments now, and we can clear everything away before looking at the display material.'

Within five minutes there was a cheerful racket of gossip and coffee cups, and Mrs Gibbons turned to Alan Lester, who was now sharing the desk with her.

'All going very well, I think,' she commented.

'Very well indeed,' Alan agreed sincerely.

Although the Henstocks' trip to London had been generally noted and approved by the residents of Lulling and Thrush Green, it was some time before Harold and Isobel heard the details of that memorable evening. They were sitting in the Shoosmiths' garden one balmy evening of early summer enjoying the scent of pinks in the border and the sharp fragrance from the Albertine rose on the wall.

'Beautiful music,' enthused Charles. '*Real* music, you know, Haydn and Vivaldi, or one of those thumpy bits from Handel that you ought to know and never do.'

'It was Bach, dear,' said Dimity. 'And Robert took us to a very good Italian restaurant just off the Strand. So welcoming the owners were. A family concern, with Papa and Mama, and I should think Grandpapa in that basket chair, wouldn't you, Charles?'

'Definitely,' agreed Charles, 'and such delicious food. It really was a great treat for us.'

'And so nice to see Dulcie Mulloy again,' added Dimity.

'So she was there,' commented Isobel, refilling glasses.

'Yes, she works in the City and met us at the restaurant.'

'By the way, Robert had more news of the Fennel family. You know that our Octavius's money came from the Lancashire cotton trade originally?'

'Yes, I remember. We wondered if he might feel guilty about it.'

'He was looking up a name in his local telephone directory in the Fs, and came across some Fennels. He was talking to his doctor a day or so later who told him that quite a few wealthy Fennels retired to the Lake District. One of the survivors was one of his patients, who lived in a hideous Victorian mock-castle built by one of his rich forebears near Windermere.'

'How extraordinary!' exclaimed Harold. 'And are they related to our Octavius? It's an unusual name.'

'Robert went to see him. Yes, he is vaguely related, I gather. He's in his nineties, a bachelor, very frail, and living in part of the old house. He was most interested in all Robert had to tell him.'

'Had he ever met Octavius?'

'No. But his father had visited Octavius several times and thought a great deal of him.'

'And what about the other Lake District Fennels?'

'Distantly connected evidently, but no contact. Different generations, and not in touch with the old man Robert met. He wants to be kept informed about our celebrations. I wonder if we should invite him?'

'Would he come? He sounds rather past travelling,' said Harold.

Charles nodded thoughtfully. 'Nevertheless, I think I will send him an invitation when I get round to sending them out. Incidentally, I have sent a copy of the parish magazine to Nathaniel's African mission station, to show them that we are celebrating their opening.'

'Good!' said Harold. 'It all sounds very exciting, and your evening was a fruitful one. What was the journey like?'

'Very simple, thanks to Robert. He met us at Paddington and took us back there after the concert. I fear we must have taken him out of his way.'

'You see,' explained Dimity, 'he insisted on taking Dulcie home to her flat in north London, after dropping us off. She said she could easily go back on the Tube, as she does every day, but Robert didn't like the idea. He was quite firm, wasn't he, Charles?'

'Indeed he was! He said he thought that women should be escorted home safely, particularly after dark. He was rather anxious about Dulcie on our first meeting at the vicarage, you may recall, because she had to set off rather late.'

'I well remember,' replied Isobel.

It was agreed that the invitations should go out early.

'It's amazing,' said Charles, 'how quickly one's diary gets filled, and after all the first of October will soon come round.'

There were not many personal invitations, for everyone in Thrush Green and Lulling had been apprised of the date and of the welcome awaiting them at the celebrations.

But Robert Wilberforce, as the person who had discovered the letters and the diary, headed the list, and Dulcie Mulloy, as a direct descendant, came next, and the aged and unseen Mr Fennel in the Lake District was also invited, and a few others.

Harold himself wrote to the head of the mission station and hoped that he or anyone else interested might be able to make the journey to join them, and offered hospitality in his own home. But somehow he doubted if anyone from so far away would undertake the trip.

The question of raising money for a modest memorial to the two men had been discussed. Charles, from the first, had felt that the offerings on the Sunday nearest 1 October should be used for such a scheme, and it had been decided to plant two trees, one for Nathaniel and the other for Octavius, as part of the celebrations.

It was a chance remark of Alan Lester's, some time after the Parent–Teacher meeting, which made Charles and Harold wonder if more could not be done, and when letters arrived from the African mission station, the three men met at the Shoosmiths' to make some plans.

'I suppose I set the ball rolling,' confessed Alan. 'I let the children send a card to the children at the mission school, telling them briefly about our festivities here. I had a long letter back from the head there, and he asked us to write regularly.'

He put a packet of leaflets about the project and the letter on the coffee table in front of them.

'I've had these, too,' said Charles, handling the leaflets, 'but my letter came later separately.'

Harold had also received a letter from the mission's head. 'They don't feel that they can send anyone on the day in question, as they will be holding their own celebration, of course, but when the head gets leave later he will come and see us, he says.'

'What's quite apparent,' said Alan, 'is their own centenary project of adding a room to the present school so that they can admit younger children. Can we afford to send them something towards that?'

'It's a nice idea,' commented Harold. 'Let's have a really rousing fundraising effort,' He looked at Charles.

'It is indeed,' said the rector thoughtfully, 'but I felt from the start that we shouldn't look upon this affair as a money-making project. That's why I sincerely hope that the church offerings on that Sunday will cover the cost of the two trees, and in any case we can supplement the sum from the Free-Will offering fund, if need be.'

'I think everyone appreciates that,' agreed Harold, 'but nevertheless I have had one or two people offering a contribution if we are collecting funds. Robert Wilberforce for one. He says that he has had such pleasure in being involved with this fresh slant on the lives of Nathaniel and Octavius. There will be others.'

'Mrs Gibbons,' added Alan, 'or I suppose I should say the Parent–Teacher Association, wants to give something to the school to celebrate the centenary, and we proposed to have a bird bath in the playground. But there might possibly be some money over.'

'I think the best thing to do,' said Charles slowly, 'would be to leave it to individuals to do as they please. No pressurizing. Perhaps a note in the parish magazine, and a box in the church and elsewhere for any donations? Let's see what sort of response we get, and we can decide then about any help towards the new schoolroom.'

'I think that's wise,' agreed Harold, 'but there's just one thing. I feel that any cash given to our own school should remain for the school's needs. If parents like to give to the boxes or at the church service, well and good, but we must not lose sight of our own centenary.'

And on this note the informal meeting broke up.

*

Thrush Green looked at its best in the summer, thought Winnie, looking from her front garden across the expanse of green to The Two Pheasants.

Mr Jones had six hanging baskets full of geraniums, lobelias and fuchsias adorning the front of the public house. In the great tub by the front door a blaze of petunias showed up against the background of creamy Cotswold stone. Winnie recalled the Christmas tree with its twinkling lights which had stood there in December, and remembered, too, how wretched she had felt with her internal troubles.

Now she felt as bonny as Mr Jones's flowers, she told herself. The sun was warm on her back as she leant over the gate. To her right the Youngs' house glowed in the dazzling light. Sunshine brought out the warm glow of the local stone; winter weather seemed to turn the buildings to a duller shade, and skies were overcast for far too much of the year for Winnie's comfort. Sometimes she looked back to the fresh charms of the holiday at Barton, and wondered if she would like to settle by the sea one day. But she knew, in her heart, that she would never leave Thrush Green.

A scarecrow figure came into view across the green, preceded by a King Charles's spaniel on a long lead. Obviously, Flossie and her mistress, Dotty Harmer, were taking a little exercise.

Winnie walked across to meet them.

A toddler was sitting on the grass beside a young girl. Winnie recognized them as part of the large Cooke family, noted in the district for fecundity and a distaste for orthodox matrimony.

But the pair were charming, Winnie thought, greeting them. They were busy making a long daisy chain. The little boy stumbled towards the blossoms starring the grass, collapsing unsteadily beside his protector (sister, mother?) while she threaded them industriously together.

They were both fair-headed, chubby-cheeked and exuded

robust health. Donald had always admired the toughness of the Cooke tribe, Winnie remembered, giving as its reason 'a fine mixture of blood'. They smiled at Winnie as she spoke to them, displaying splendid teeth which Winnie envied.

Flossie now bounded forward, at the extreme end of her long leash, and began to lick the child's face.

'Ah! Dear pussy!' cooed the boy. 'Nice pussy!'

He attempted to feed the excited dog with a fistful of daisies.

'It's a *dog*, dear,' said Dotty approaching. 'Not a *cat*.'

The child smiled disarmingly. 'Pussy!' he repeated.

'No, dear,' persisted Dotty, who disliked inaccuracy. 'You can tell by the coat. A cat has *fur*! This dog has *hair*.'

'He don't know no different,' explained his sister (mother?). 'He calls all of 'em "Pussy", even our tortoise, and Perce Hodge's cows.'

'Ah well,' said Dotty indulgently, 'he is young yet.'

The two old friends entered Winnie's garden and sat down to enjoy a rest and the scent of summer flowers. Bumblebees fumbled at the velvet lips of the snapdragons, and a blackbird foraged busily for fodder in the border.

'Tell me,' said Winnie, 'how is the book getting on?'

Dotty sighed. 'I am finding it very heavy going. Ever since Harold Shoosmith said that it was too short I have felt rather low about it, and as I told you, the accounts about my father from former pupils at the grammar school are really rather disappointing. At times I found them *scurrilous*. I mean, we all know that he saw no harm in correcting a boy, but I am quite sure that some of the writers *exaggerated* the physical discipline he imposed. I really *cannot* include some of their accounts, and I fear there may be jealousy if I use some and not others.'

Winnie doubted this, but simply offered sympathy with Dotty's problems. 'I should give up the idea of getting a publisher to take it,' she advised her. 'Much better to write the whole thing yourself, no matter how short it seems, then get it printed privately. Better still, turn it into a decent-length article for a local paper. It would reach the readers who knew him and would be interested.'

Dotty nodded. 'I must confess,' she admitted, 'that I was so looking forward to a bound copy of my work, but I suppose I must give up the idea. Life is full of disappointments I find, particularly as I get older.'

'Cheer up,' said Winnie. 'Come and choose a lettuce. We've so many that half of them have bolted.'

'Could I have them for my hens?' cried Dotty, literary disappointments forgotten. 'The dear girls love lettuce, and I could easily have a few of the good leaves for my lunch, and not rob you of a perfectly good lettuce. I was brought up to be *frugal*, you know.'

'You are to have the very best lettuce I can find for your lunch,' said Winnie firmly, leading the way to the vegetable garden. 'Let the hens practise frugality with the bolted ones.'

*

The fine weather continued, and one hot day succeeded another. On one of these sunny evenings Harold Shoosmith had a telephone call from Robert Wilberforce. He sounded excited.

'I called on my friend Frederick Fennel today,' he said. 'He is delighted to be invited to the festivities, but is afraid he is not up to the journey. He has written to Charles, I gather. But that's not all.'

'How d'you mean?'

'He was a boy when Octavius died in 1912, but his father was evidently in Thrush Green, staying with Octavius a year or two before that, and he attended the interment of Nathaniel. Octavius took the service. This must have been in 1910 or 1911.'

'I'm amazed. Was it Octavius who had the body shipped back from Africa?'

'It was indeed, according to Frederick's memories of his father's account. Octavius got in touch with the Dr Maurice at the mission station, and the body was treated with aromatic drugs and spices – embalmed evidently, and with great skill by the Africans – then shipped home to Bristol. It was winter when it arrived, and Frederick's father stayed longer than he expected at Thrush Green rectory, because there was heavy snow. In fact, there was snow still on the ground when Octavius took the funeral.'

'I find this very touching,' said Harold, looking across the sunlit green to the churchyard, and envisaging the black and white winter scene so many years ago.

'I thought you would be interested,' said Robert. 'It has been wonderful to talk to the old boy, and the celebrations have really given him as great an interest as they have us. I wish he could make the journey, but frankly it is out of the question. Still, as you can see, his mind is as clear as ever, even if he is frail of body.'

They talked a little longer, then Harold returned to Isobel in the garden, and told her all about this further evidence of Octavius's affection for his younger friend.

'It's a sad story,' said Isobel. 'Poor Octavius, standing in the snow by the grave of a friend.'

'It reminded me of the burial of Mozart in a snowstorm,' replied Harold. 'All the mourners turned back, they say.'

'Well, Nathaniel had some mourners,' comforted Isobel, 'and a private grave, not the common pit that Mozart was thrown into. When you think about it – the shipment home, the decent burial, the sincere grief and the respect that came to both men – it makes a heartening story, not a tragic one.'

And Harold, seeing the wisdom of this, agreed.

At Thrush Green school preparations for the Victorian day were going ahead with all the excitement and set-backs that usually accompany a school project.

Some of the ancient desks had been tracked down and were to be delivered to the school in good time for the first of October. Only the chapel people were slightly less obliging as Bright Hour took place on the Tuesday preceding the great day, and the desks would be needed to support the chapel china and tea urn as usual. However, Mrs Jones, wife of the landlord of The Two Pheasants, said that she would see that the two desks were brought up after Bright Hour, and woe betide any person who stood in her way.

Alan Lester had no doubt that Mrs Jones would be a reliable assistant in his endeavours, and concentrated on the many other aspects of the celebration.

As might be expected, the question of costume was the biggest headache. The girls were quite excited and co-operative about their attire, bringing various garments for approval and comparing notes on length of skirts, the necessity for aprons, shawls and so on. It was the boys who were awkward and self-conscious.

'We shan't half look clowns,' Alan heard one say.

'Soppy idea,' agreed his companion. 'I reckon I'll stay home that day.'

It was Bill Hooper who saved the day. The biggest boy in the school, and acknowledged king of the playground, he had also been included in a local junior football team when a player had fallen ill at the last minute. Consequently, Bill was something of a hero, and due deference was paid to him by his companions.

When the question of the boys' costumes cropped up, he casually mentioned that his grandfather, a tailor in Lulling, was making him a Norfolk suit for the occasion.

An unusual hush fell upon the classroom, much to Alan Lester's amusement.

'It's a bit of tweed I chose myself,' went on Bill, amidst stunned silence. 'The gamekeepers over Nidden way used to have suits of it in the old days. That was before the place was sold. My grandpa always helped to make their suits.'

'I should like to see it,' said Alan. 'It should look very well on you.'

'If you like,' went on Bill, flattered by the attention, 'I'll wear it to school one day, before October, I mean.'

'Splendid!' said Alan. 'And that's enough about our costumes. Take out your atlases.'

From then on there was little complaint from the male members of the school. In fact, there seemed to be mild enthusiasm as spotted neckerchieves and Eton collars were discussed, and the chance of getting someone's hobnail boots was debated.

All in all, Alan thought, the school was getting truly involved with this portrayal of school life as experienced by their grandparents and great-grandparents in this selfsame building, and when Miss Robinson and the young probationer were heard to say that they proposed to wear stockings *with garters* instead of their usual tights, he felt assured of the complete success of the great day ahead.

9. GETTING READY

Summer that year was long and very hot, interspersed with violent thunderstorms which flattened much of the corn. Nevertheless, the farmers had an early harvest in a dry spell, and were hard put to find anything much to grumble about.

As she dressed one August morning, Winnie Bailey looked across the green to the distant fields towards Lulling Woods. In some the golden stubble still gleamed, but already the ploughs had been at work in neighbouring fields, although the corn had only been collected, it seemed, a day or two earlier.

There were plenty of young pheasants about but, looking at the distant stubble fields, Winnie remembered how plentiful the native partridge had been when she had come as a young bride to live in this same house. Now that the fields had been cleared and so quickly ploughed or drilled ready for the next crop, the number of partridge had dwindled. Such a pity, thought Winnie, who had always had a soft spot for these squat plump little birds. She had been told that they mated for life, and that they were exemplary parents. Winnie approved of both constancy and family commitment, and regretted the demise of such charming birds.

She leant from her window to survey the green. It was the time of day which she most enjoyed, particularly at this stage of the year, when dew was heavy and spangled spiders' webs shimmered on the hedges. Soon there would be mushrooms and blackberries about, and the sharp blue-bloomed sloes which Donald had enjoyed picking for the sloe gin he made every autumn. Soon, too, the conkers would be falling from the horse chestnut trees near by, and already a pale carpet made of the lime flowers and bracts lay under the trees by the church. Albert would not approve, thought Winnie.

As if on cue, the old man emerged from his cottage door, and stood in his shirt sleeves looking up at the sky, as if daring it to rain. Even at this stage of the day he wore his old greasy cap on the back of his head. Winnie wondered if he wore it at the breakfast table. Even in bed, perhaps?

She heard Jenny moving about in the kitchen and, idle conjectures shelved, went downstairs to join her.

With the school holidays in full swing, there was little that Alan Lester could do in the way of preparing for the school's part in the celebrations.

The timetable for the Victorian day had been devised and rehearsed for timing and effect. A number of relics had been collected, including several of the original desks and some splendid old photographs of classes of the 1890s which people had lent, and which Alan proposed to hang round the walls. It was interesting to see how many of the boys, and the girls, too, had close-cropped heads. Fashion, wondered Alan? Or, more practically, prevention of head lice? Possibly the aftermath of ringworm?

The girls all appeared to have worn white pinafores, black stockings and laced or buttoned boots. The boys' costumes were more varied: Norfolk jackets, jerseys with collars, coats and trousers obviously handed down from larger brothers, and here and there an Eton collar gleaming among the subfusc ensemble.

There were one or two ragged children to be seen, but on the whole, Alan thought, studying those long-dead faces through a magnifying glass, they appeared to have been a sturdy lot, toughened by plenty of exercise tramping to and from school, and field work for the bigger boys whenever the local farmer was in need of extra hands.

Perhaps country children had always had a slightly easier life than their town contemporaries. Alan remembered his father telling him about barefoot boys, fighting over half a loaf, whom he had seen in the dockyard area of the city where he had lived as a child. In those bleak streets there were no apples to scrump, no blackberries on hedges, no young turnips to pull secretly from a field's edge, and too many sharp eyes looking to catch a wrongdoer.

Looking across the green from his study window, he could see his two daughters playing with their school friends by the swings near the church. All the children were laughing, their hair streaming in the wind, their teeth and eyes gleaming, their limbs straight and strong. They might have been a different race altogether from the crop-headed few who gazed from the old photographs.

Indeed, thought Alan, there were many reasons for celebration.

Down at Barton-on-Sea Dorothy and Agnes were also looking forward to the Thrush Green celebrations.

They were busy with jam-making, for their two plum trees, thriving in the hot summer, had produced a bumper crop, and although Agnes was not over-fond of plum jam, Dorothy had insisted on making as much as they could.

'It's so *useful* for bazaars and things,' said Dorothy, bustling about with jam jars and little waxed discs which fluttered to the kitchen floor in profusion. 'You know how pleased the vicar was with that redcurrant jelly I made. "Ruby red", he called it. "Ruby red, and a real jewel." I thought it most apt.'

Agnes, standing over a hot stove, doing her best to fish out plum stones with a spoon, to be deposited on an old enamel plate steaming near by, thought it was a jolly sight easier making jelly than trying to catch elusive plum stones, the present task, which Dorothy had allotted her. She did her best to put this unworthy thought aside, and Dorothy's next words helped a little.

'I always start thinking of the new school year at about this time,' she said, rescuing some jam-pot covers from the floor.

'So do I,' agreed Agnes.

'And I must say, I really relish the thought of not having to go back,' added Dorothy.

'I'd rather like to,' confessed Agnes, pursuing a particularly slippery stone. 'The new babies were so sweet.'

'You were always so patient with the newcomers,' said Dorothy. 'I must admit that I really could not have coped with the reception class – all those tears and trips to the lavatories. No, I like them rather more *mental* and a little less *physical*. What on earth is that cat doing?'

The two ladies suspended their operations to gaze down at Tim, who was under the kitchen table. To their horror they saw that the cat had his paw firmly on a small and terrified mouse.

'Timmy,' said Dorothy, in her headmistress voice. 'Take that thing outside.'

The cat growled.

Dorothy snatched up the washing-up mop, and bent down. 'Timmy, be *reasonable*!' she adjured the animal. 'We simply can't have a mouse in here. It's unsanitary.'

'*Insanitary*,' corrected Agnes automatically, 'and in any case Tim might get splashed with hot jam. And the mouse too, for that matter.'

Dorothy, red-faced, straightened up. 'This is no time for humanitarian nonsense,' she puffed. 'Let's just shoo both of them outside.'

She opened the door into the garden and Agnes, abandoning her jam, bent down to persuade Tim to relinquish his captive.

In true cat fashion, he strolled casually away to the open door, and the mouse fled to take refuge under the refrigerator.

'*Really!*' said Dorothy, much exasperated. 'How typical! Now we shall have the impossible task of getting that mouse out.'

Agnes took charge. 'I'm turning the heat down, and making us coffee. Leave the door open, dear, and it's bound to run out eventually. It's time we had a rest in the sitting-room.'

There was a thump at the front door, and Dorothy went to collect the letters.

By the time they were ensconced in the peace of the sitting-room, with their coffee and post, the friends were calm again.

'Look,' said Dorothy, holding up a card. 'It's a proper invitation to the school on the first of October.'

'I've one, too,' said Agnes. 'How nice of Alan Lester to send separate ones!'

'Very extravagant,' said Dorothy, taking a biscuit, but she sounded pleased, and they began to discuss their plans for the journey, and the all-important problem of *what to wear*.

Out in the kitchen a quaking mouse emerged from its

hide-out and made a dash for the fresh air. From his perch on the sunny rooftop of the garden shed, Tim ceased to wash his paws and watched the mouse with a languid eye.

Really rather a bore, this mousing, on a hot morning.

The new school term at Thrush Green began in the usual back-to-school weather of cloudless skies and warm sunshine, causing much irritation to those who had spent a great deal of money taking a holiday on the rainswept coasts of this island or, even worse, at the far more expensive and even more weatherbeaten resorts overseas.

The first priority was, of course, the final preparations for the great day.

Alan Lester, as an experienced head teacher, had no doubt that all would go well on the day. He also knew that there would be untold hazards to overcome before the dawn of 1 October.

Bill Hooper, true to his word, appeared a week or two before celebration day resplendent in his tweed Norfolk suit. His schoolfellows were duly impressed, and he strode round the classroom amidst awe and admiration.

There was no doubt about it: Bill's unseen grandfather still knew how to cut and sew, and Alan blessed him for smoothing his path on this occasion, for although no other boy could aspire to such sartorial perfection, at least they all looked forward to parading in garments which they would have scorned before Bill's and his grandfather's initiative.

The girls had been enthusiastic about their dressing-up from the first. Alan and Miss Robinson had planned the general look of the rooms, and had been almost overwhelmed by the amount of bric-à-brac sent in by parents and well-wishers.

But a hindrance to progress had been Mrs Gibbons.

From the first, Alan had realized that her position on the Parent–Teacher committee would give her every excuse for interfering, and he was prepared.

It was unfortunate that the lady took to entering the schoolroom unbidden to make her suggestions and criticisms. Alan Lester knew, as well as she did, that any confrontation before the children put her at an advantage, and he was quick to point out that it was not convenient to discuss plans during school hours.

'I simply wanted to have a look at the *setting*,' protested Mrs Gibbons, waving a hand. 'I had an idea which I think could improve the early part of the proceedings. It concerns the piano, and the children marching to their places.'

'That is already arranged,' Alan told her, with one eye on two giggling girls at the back of the class. 'Miss Robinson and I have been into it thoroughly.'

'But have you chosen the hymns? I have been looking through *Hymns Ancient and Modern* and *Songs of Praise*—'

Here Alan led her firmly to the door.

'I really cannot discuss it now. I will telephone you after school and perhaps we can talk about things then.'

'We certainly will,' replied Mrs Gibbons emphatically, and went, seething, into the lobby.

There had been one or two other visitations, but on the whole she kept her attacks until after school hours. They ranged from strong disapproval of the sort of food the children would bring to school for their Victorian snack, to the fact that the whole school would go to the church service on the morning of 1 October.

'I feel quite sure,' she told Alan, 'that the chapel children would *never* have entered St Andrew's. It is quite wrong that they should go on this occasion.'

Alan explained, as patiently as he could, that this particular act of worship had nothing to do with the Victorian day celebrations, but was a contribution by the school – a Church of England school, he emphasized – to the general honouring of Nathaniel Patten and Octavius Fennel.

The lady, though still antagonistic, gave way grudgingly.

'It will be rather a relief,' said Alan to his wife, as he replaced the telephone, 'to get back to the humdrum of daily teaching when these celebrations are over.'

One morning towards the end of September, Charles Henstock received a letter which gave him surprise and delight.

It was beautifully typed on crisp white writing paper and the address was embossed, something which the rector rarely saw these days.

It read:

> Dear Mr Henstock,
>   I wish that I could accept your very kind invitation to the festivities at Thrush Green on 1 October, but ill-health prevents me from travelling.
>   My young friend Robert Wilberforce has kept me informed

of the plans to honour Mr Nathaniel Patten and my kinsman the Reverend Octavius Fennel. I have followed the proposals with great interest, as you may imagine.

I understand that it is hoped to send a donation toward the building of an extra room at the African mission school, and should like to contribute. Robert Wilberforce is attending your celebrations, he tells me, and I shall entrust him with my donation then.

I shall be with you in spirit on 1 October and feel sure that all your endeavours will be successful.

    Yours sincerely,
    Frederick Fennel

Half an hour later, Charles rang Harold to tell him about the proposed donation.

'That's most kind of him,' said Harold, 'and will be very welcome. I must admit, Charles, that contributions are not coming in as I had hoped, despite your note in the parish magazine.'

'I felt that might be the case,' said Charles. 'There are so many claims on people's purses, and charity begins at home, of course.'

'Naturally, and I believe that our school fund is receiving more support than Nathaniel's, which, I suppose, is only to be expected. I feel rather a fool, though, looking back at all the high hopes I had of raising a goodly sum for Nathaniel.'

'Don't worry,' Charles said. 'There's still time.' But was there?

'By the way,' added Harold, 'a warning! Mrs Gibbons has a new idea for adding to the glory of the great day, and may be coming to tell you about it.'

'Oh dear!'

'Oh dear, it certainly is. She thinks it might be nice to have large photographs of Nathaniel and Octavius propped up on their graves in Thrush Green churchyard during the celebrations. The Gauleiter would be glad to make the enlargements from the photographs we have.'

'The Gauleiter?'

'Sorry. I mean Mr Gibbons. Just my facetious name for him.'

'But I don't like the idea at all,' cried Charles pathetically.

'Neither would anyone else,' Harold assured him. 'I told her that she was trying to turn an English country churchyard into an Italian cemetery.'

'Oh dear,' repeated Charles. 'Was she offended?'

'*Very!*' said Harold, with intense satisfaction.

'Well, thank you for warning me. Now I am going to write to Frederick Fennel.'

'It's wonderful news,' said Harold, 'and I wish he were well enough to join us.'

Towards the end of September the wind turned from the quarter which had given the sunny clear spell, to the south-west. Grey clouds lowered over Thrush Green, and although the rain that fell from them was welcomed by everyone, and particularly by the gardeners, it did not bode well for the day of celebration to come.

It grew chilly, too, in the evenings and Winnie began to look ahead.

'I'm getting my overseas Christmas parcels ready in good time this year,' she told Jenny. 'And we ought to think about having our flu inoculations, and checking the state of the coal cellar.'

'Well, I've done that,' Jenny told her. 'Summer prices for the coal. I don't know as I'm all that keen on a flu jab this year.'

'Now, Jenny,' began Winnie, in her doctor's-wife voice, 'I'm sure these jabs really help.'

'Nothing more than faith healing, I reckon.'

Winnie pondered on the comment. 'Faith healing or not,' she pronounced, 'I've never had flu really badly since I started them.'

It so happened that the next morning she saw John Lovell arrive, in driving rain, and hurry into the surgery. She slipped on a coat and hurried across the drive to catch him before his patients arrived.

It always gave her a feeling of comfort to enter Donald's old place of work. She approved of the familiar central table with magazines neatly set out in rows, the vase of garden flowers on the mantelpiece, and on the wall the photograph of Donald himself which John had placed there.

'Am I a nuisance?' said Winnie when John opened the door from the waiting-room to his surgery. 'It's just about making a date for a flu jab.'

'Never a nuisance,' John told her, turning over the leaves of a diary on his desk. 'What about a Wednesday towards the end of October?'

'I'd better let Jenny make her own arrangements,' said Winnie, watching him fill in an appointment for herself. 'She's a bit anti-jab at the moment, but I think she'll come round to the idea.'

'And how are you feeling? No after-affects of Paterson's work?'

'I had a twinge or two soon after the operation,' Winnie confessed, 'but they have been few and far between, and the last one was weeks ago.'

'It's probably just the internal scar healing,' said John, 'but would you like me to have a look? Better still, I could send you back to Philip Paterson if you're worried.'

'I honestly don't think it's necessary, but if I get any pain at all I promise to tell you.'

There were sounds of footsteps and voices, and Winnie moved towards the door.

'I mustn't keep you any longer.' She looked at Donald's photograph. 'I always liked that photo of Donald. He looks thoroughly pleased with life, doesn't he?'

'I think he was,' replied John seriously. 'He had a worthwhile job, lots of friends and a splendid wife.'

Winnie smiled at the compliment.

'It's good to have him there,' went on John. 'The old people like to remember him. As I do, too. He was always an example to me of what a good doctor should be.'

The outer door opened and a blast of damp air blew in.

'Dratted rain!' said a country voice, and Winnie hurried past the first of John's patients to regain her home.

Dorothy and Agnes set off for Thrush Green on the last day of September. They had been invited to stay at the Shoosmiths for a week, but Dorothy had decided that they should go back on the day after the celebrations.

'We both thought we should have time on our hands when we retired,' she explained to Isobel on the telephone. 'But as it is we seem to be always busy. We are giving a coffee morning in aid of the RSPB on the Saturday, and I'm on the flower rota at church for that weekend, and Agnes has an appointment with the chiropodist, and that's how it goes!'

Isobel was sympathetic, and Harold, when he heard the news, was secretly relieved. Much as he respected their old neighbours, he found Dorothy's setting of the world to rights somewhat tiring, but he kept these thoughts to himself.

In truth, he had other worries. The rector's note about donations in the parish magazine had had little response. The amount for the annexe to Nathaniel's school was less than a hundred pounds, and although Harold proposed to add his own contribution, there was no doubt in his mind that the final sum would be insignificant.

He understood the position. Thrush Green school had prior claim, and Alan Lester would certainly have more than enough for the bird bath envisaged.

He realized now that he had been absurdly optimistic. In his enthusiasm for anything connected with Nathaniel, he had been over-ambitious. As a proud man he was now suffering secret humiliation, and it hurt.

However, he comforted himself, Charles was right. Charity begins at home, and that was as it should be.

The rain fell relentlessly, and Dorothy drove with the windscreen wipers working full time. In places there were floods across the road, and the rivers of Hampshire, Berkshire and Oxfordshire, which had dwindled dramatically throughout the long summer, were now being rapidly replenished and flowing with their usual speed and volume.

They stopped in Lulling, and Dorothy braved the rain to enter a florist's near The Fuchsia Bush in order to buy a magnificent hibiscus plant for Isobel. Agnes held it carefully on her knees as they passed the familiar sights then climbed the steep hill to their old home.

'Stop the car for a minute,' cried Agnes. 'I must just have a look at dear old Thrush Green.'

Dorothy obliged, and turned off the engine. In the sudden silence of the car they became conscious of the outside noises.

Rain pattered on the roof above them. Drops dripped from Mr Jones's brave flower baskets, and little rivulets gurgled their way towards the hill which dipped to the town. The grass of the green looked soggy and the chestnut trees drooped with the weight of wet leaves.

'Dear, oh dear!' said Dorothy at last, breaking the silence. 'It's a sad sight. What will it be like tomorrow?'

'It will be absolutely splendid,' Agnes told her, undaunted. 'Rain or shine, we shall *celebrate*, and I don't care if it *snows*, Dorothy, as long as we're at Thrush Green.'

Smiling at such enthusiasm Dorothy started the car again and they splashed the few yards to their destination.

10. Celebration

Little Agnes Fogerty awoke during the night. By the clock in the Shoosmiths' spare bedroom she saw that it said ten to three and, as always at that time, thought of Rupert Brooke and honey, before making her way to the window.

Thrush Green glittered under a full moon which was hidden every now and again by ragged clouds which rushed across from the west. Puddles gleamed in the fitful light, and the trees tossed their branches, sending raindrops sparkling to the sodden grass. The windowpane was spangled with silver drops, but the rain itself had stopped.

Perhaps, thought Agnes, returning to her bed, this wind will dry things. In any case the bonfire should burn splendidly.

And with this comforting thought, she fell asleep again.

She was not the only person in Thrush Green to take particular note of the weather during the hours of darkness, and by morning there were very few who were not peering through windows, or standing in their gardens, assessing the chances of a dry day for the celebrations.

To be sure, things did not look very hopeful. The wind still roared in the trees, the puddles shivered under its onslaught, and Willie Marchant, the postman, was tacking back and forth uphill from Lulling against a powerful cross-wind.

But in the east the sky seemed lighter, and by nine o'clock

a watery sun occasionally cast a gleam between the scudding clouds.

At the school the children were in a state of great excitement. Any departure from routine, as all teachers know, is welcomed by pupils and staff alike, and although the dress rehearsal had taken place on the Tuesday, amidst much general ribaldry about appearances of costume and demeanour, the actual day brought even more noise and disruption to the metamorphosed classrooms.

Alan Lester's command of his troops, however, ensured suitable decorum from all as they prepared to walk in twos across to the church at ten o'clock.

Charles and Dimity arrived in good time, but Dimity's attention was divided between the ceremony to come and the lunch preparations she had left behind.

Dulcie Mulloy and Robert Wilberforce were driving down together from London for the service, and had been invited to lunch at the vicarage.

Harold and Isobel had also been invited, and as soon as Dimity heard that Dorothy Watson and Agnes Fogerty would be staying, they too were included in the invitation.

Had she forgotten to put sugar in the plum crumble? wondered Dimity, agreeing with Ella Bembridge that the wind had dropped a little. Should she have done a dish of potatoes? Men ate rather a lot, and Robert Wilberforce looked as though he ate heartily.

She took her place halfway down the church, and there was the sound of children being marshalled on the gravel outside the west door.

While they awaited the entry of the school children, Dimity cast an appraising eye round the congregation. St Andrew's was rarely as full as this. There was Winnie across the aisle, sharing a pew with Dotty Harmer and her niece Connie, and Connie's husband Kit.

Percy Hodge and his wife Gladys sat behind, and Dimity appreciated the fact that such a staunch chapel-goer as Gladys had come to this church to give thanks for the lives of Nathaniel and Octavius. What's more, thought Dimity, she has persuaded Percy to come, too, although she suspected correctly that Percy would be quite agreeable to go to any religious establishment if Gladys told him to, for Percy really had no religious convictions of any kind, as she well knew. Nevertheless, it was good to see him and many others of the same sort, coming to do honour to the long-dead, and on a Thursday morning, too.

In the front left-hand pew she saw Robert Wilberforce and Dulcie Mulloy. They had been ushered into this prominent position by Albert Piggott (now hovering by the west door to make sure that the children wiped their shoes), on the command of the rector of Thrush Green who had pointed out to Albert the importance of these two visitors to the celebrations.

At this point the school entered, looking both uncommonly devout and demure in its Victorian garb. There was a rustle of movement as people turned to watch them file to the pews at the right-hand front of the church, and Alan Lester, bringing up the rear, felt a glow of pride at his pupils' appearance and behaviour.

They had hardly settled when the organ crashed into a joyous noise, and the choir and vicar processed from the west door down the aisle, leading the congregation in the hearty singing of 'Christ whose glory fills the skies'.

How right, thought Dimity, to choose a hymn whose words were by Charles Wesley! It was well known that John Wesley had preached on the green outside this church, and commonly believed that Charles, too, had occasionally accompanied his more famous brother here.

The service continued, and Charles Henstock gave a moving address about the occasion. He spoke of the mission school so far away, and yet so close to their hearts. He reminded them of Christ's words quoted by Octavius Fennel: 'Suffer the little children to come unto me', and also the exhortation from Ecclesiasticus: 'Let us now praise famous men', which they were obeying today.

He also said how grateful they all were to Robert Wilberforce, whose public-spirited action in bringing Nathaniel's letters and Octavius's diary to light had made these celebrations possible, and had moreover, been instrumental in bringing Nathaniel's great-granddaughter to Thrush Green to join in their rejoicing.

After the address all rose to sing:

> *Let us all praise famous men*
> *They of little showing*
> *For their work continueth*
> *And their work continueth,*
> *Broad and deep continueth*
> *Greater than their knowing.*

As they sang, the sun sent a few half-hearted rays through the windows on the south side of St Andrew's, and cheered all the congregation.

After the final blessing, the school children walked out first and took their places in the churchyard as rehearsed. The adults followed them, then came Dulcie Mulloy and Robert Wilberforce, each bearing a magnificent wreath which had been standing in the porch.

The gathering moved to one end of the churchyard where stood the graves of the two friends.

Some years earlier, the bulk of the tombstones had been

moved to the sides of the graveyard, allowing easier use of the mower by young Cooke, and easier maintenance, such as it was, by Albert Piggott. But at one end of the churchyard grew several lime trees which drooped their branches over the line of graves by that wall, and it had been decided to leave those tombs undisturbed. Among them were those of Nathaniel and Octavius, and after a short prayer, Dulcie, as direct descendant, advanced to put her wreath on Nathaniel's grave.

Robert Wilberforce performed the same honour for Octavius Fennel, and the service ended.

The children were ushered back to school by the three teachers, ready for the next part of their anniversary celebrations, and their elders lingered by the church gate to discuss the service, the improving weather and, of course, the immediate news of Thrush Green.

Dotty Harmer, wearing a hat which could only have come from a jumble sale or charity shop, and might have been new in the 1930s, put a restraining hand on Winnie's arm.

'What a celebration! And I have a private one of my own.'

Winnie had a twinge of apprehension. What now? Had Dotty discovered yet another allegedly edible autumn fungus which she was turning into some fearsome comestible ready for distribution to her friends? She was already concocting a white lie about the delicate state of her digestion since the gall bladder operation, when she was relieved to hear that Dotty was talking about the biography she was writing about the formidable Mr Harmer, late of Lulling Grammar School.

'It's going to be *published*, my dear,' cried Dotty. 'Isn't that wonderful?'

'Wonderful!' echoed Winnie. 'Who has taken it?'

'The county magazine. You know, that thing that comes out monthly. It was Harold who suggested it. They are running a series called "Local Men of Influence", and the editor rang me himself.'

'But isn't it rather long for an article in a magazine?' queried Winnie.

'Yes, it is,' admitted Dotty, 'but he is going to suggest some cuts, and there will be a photograph of Father, and one of me at the top. The photographer came last week and spent *hours* snapping away at me in the garden. So exciting!' Dotty beamed like a child at the pantomime.

'Well, I'm absolutely delighted, Dotty. You've worked so hard, it deserves to be printed.'

'Such a nice young man, the photographer,' continued Dotty as they walked away from the church. 'No tie, of course, but he had one gold earring. I suppose he had lost the other, but when I expressed concern he only laughed. I gave him a pot of my strawberry preserve.'

'Oh, that couldn't hurt him,' said Winnie, and then thought that that involuntary cry of relief might seem a little tactless in the circumstances. However, she decided, as she walked alone towards her home, Dotty's present state of euphoria would protect her from taking umbrage.

At the school everything was ready for the influx of parents and friends. It was an Open Day from now on, and a number of local people came straight over from St Andrew's to enjoy the spectacle of a Victorian school.

The staff and children had achieved a wonderful transformation, largely by removing the colourful friezes and the other bright objects of modem education.

A blackboard propped on an easel bore the precepts, written in Alan Lester's best copperplate hand-writing:

> *Cleanliness is next to godliness.*
> *Do the work which is to hand.*
> *Obedience is a child's first duty.*
> *God watcheth over all.*

The bigger children were copying this work into lined exercise books using wooden pen holders with steel nibs. The younger ones were squeaking slate pencils on slate boards, or using sticks of chalk on individual blackboards about a foot square. These relics of the past had been lent by local museums and interested elderly friends who had dug them out of attics or dusty toy boxes, but one slate board, it was claimed by its owner, was still in regular use, propped in her porch, as a means of communicating with the tradesmen when she was not at home.

At twelve o'clock-work stopped and the children took out the lunches they had brought from home. These they ate in the playground to save crumbs in the classroom, for only in very severe weather were the Victorian pupils allowed into the lobby during dinner hour. A pail of drinking water and an enamel mug by it stood on the lobby floor to supply drinks, for there was no piped water at Thrush Green at that time.

During the afternoon, friends of the school watched the infants creating a long chain of bright chrysanthemum flowers intended to hang around the neck of Nathaniel Patten's bronze statue outside on the green.

This was being created amidst great excitement (and some frustration by those rebelling against their constricting Victorian clothes), like a giant daisy-chain, and was the children's own idea of paying tribute to the man who had loved children both in Thrush Green and Africa. Many a local garden had been raided for this garland, and the effect was stunning.

On a side table were displayed some of the toys which Harold Shoosmith had seen in the Lovelocks' loft. Some were Edwardian, such as the Russian egg brought back by Octavius, but there were two beautiful Victorian dolls which the sisters had inherited, a clockwork mouse and a child's wooden wheelbarrow. The Lovelocks' own dolls' house had also been sent up, for although it was not Victorian, it was in the fine tradition of 'baby houses' and a joy for the children and their parents to behold.

It was Harold who had mentioned the many trunks in the loft to Alan Lester. Would they hold untold treasures of Victorian clothes? A young and nimble friend of the sisters had been sent up to investigate for the school children, but there was nothing among the mouldering remains fit to wear, except a black straw bonnet, trimmed with jet, which none of the Thrush Green school girls could be persuaded to wear.

Along one wall were pinned the letters of the alphabet in capitals and small type, painstakingly executed by Miss Robinson over many an evening. This sight was greeted with much enthusiasm by the onlookers, which surprised the teacher, until she heard one mother remark to another:

'My schooldays coincided with a complete ban on teaching the alphabet, and I have a terrible time finding anything in the telephone directory.'

'I reckon the Victorians could teach us a thing or two about the three Rs,' agreed her friend.

While the school children ate their bread and cheese, or bread and cold bacon at Thrush Green school (supplemented, luckily, by a real school dinner soon after), there was a much more festive occasion being enjoyed at Lulling vicarage.

The sun had emerged but the air was chilly with a hint of autumn on the way.

'But you must have a look at the garden,' Charles had said when drinks were over, and Dimity had departed to the kitchen to see about the dishing-up of lunch.

Obediently, the guests followed Charles into the garden, and indeed the flower borders were in fine form with dahlias, Japanese anemones, late marigolds, hardy fuchsias and Michaelmas daisies making a riot of mixed colours and attracting plenty of butterflies into the bargain.

'Now look, Agnes,' commanded Dorothy, stopping by a low rose bush, 'this is exactly what we need under the front windows.'

The company stopped to admire the plant, and various suggestions were exchanged about its name.

'Charles!' called Harold, but the vicar had hurried ahead with Dulcie and Robert to the greenhouse at the end of the garden. Speculation continued among the group left behind.

'My geraniums have been quite outstanding this year,' said Charles to his guests, when they were in the welcome shelter of the greenhouse. 'I came across a wonderful pelargonium called Aztec, and I've taken lots of cuttings, and I have put aside half a dozen for you.'

'How nice of you,' said Dulcie.

'You will need to keep them under cover through the winter,' said Charles, busy with pots. 'I know the Lake District can be very cold.'

'I have a small conservatory,' said Robert.

'And have you?' asked Charles of Dulcie.

'Well, no, but I shall cherish them on my windowsill.'

'In fact,' said Robert firmly, 'Dulcie will keep them in *my* conservatory.'

'Indeed?' said Charles, puzzled, as he looked from face to face, a flower pot in each hand.

'We are getting married in December,' said Robert, taking Dulcie's hand.

'Oh, my dears!' cried Charles, his chubby face growing pink. 'What news! What wonderful news!'

His hands were trembling with excitement, and Dulcie removed the flower pots from him and replaced them on the slatted bench. It was the same competent manner in which he remembered her dealing with a cabbage she was cutting up, as a child long ago, in her mother's kitchen in Wales.

'We became engaged last week,' Dulcie said, 'and first of all we thought of telephoning you, but it seemed so much nicer to tell you ourselves.'

'We owe so much to you,' said Robert. 'We met here first, you remember.'

'And we wondered,' went on Dulcie, 'if you would be willing to take part in the marriage service. It will be in my parish church, but our vicar is most enthusiastic about your taking part.'

'I should count it a great honour,' Charles told them. 'In December, you say?'

'I wish it could be next week,' Robert told him, 'but Dulcie has to go with her boss to a business conference in Boston,

Massachusetts, at the end of November. Also she will be training her junior to take over her duties at the office, so I've simply got to be patient.'

'How I wish I could marry you here at my church in Lulling,' cried Charles.

'It would have been lovely,' agreed Dulcie, 'but you see Tom Evans, our vicar, has been so kind to me, and was marvellous with my mother all though her last illness and of course it is right that I should go to my own parish church—'

'Of course, of course,' Charles hastened to agree. 'And I shall look forward very much to taking part in the ceremony.'

At this point, his other guests arrived, agog with enquiries about the name of the rose which Dorothy admired. At the same time, there was the sound of a hand bell being energetically swung by Dimity who was awaiting her visitors.

'May I tell them?' whispered Charles to Robert and Dulcie as they all trooped back to the house.

'Of course,' smiled Dulcie.

Dimity had prepared a lunch which needed little last-minute attention. She had made a chicken and asparagus quiche for the main course, with a side dish of sliced home-cooked gammon and hard-boiled eggs, and a vast salad. Late raspberries and cream were to follow, and she had also made a plum crumble which had cooked alongside the quiche.

The evening before, when the cold rain lashed Lulling and Thrush Green, Dimity had become concerned about her proposed meal. Wasn't it a little *bleak*?

She departed to the kitchen, leaving Charles to watch a television programme about inter-planetary warfare which might have appealed to prep-school boys, Dimity supposed, but which she deplored. Charles seemed to be entirely engrossed, and she left him while she made enough chicken soup for a dozen, let alone the eight guests expected, and later went to bed content with the knowledge that tomorrow's first course could stand up to any Cotswold cold which the day might bring.

It was while she was dispensing this nourishment that the vicar said: 'Before you take up your spoons, I must tell you of another cause we have today for celebration.'

The Shoosmiths and their guests looked at him hopefully. Dimity, too, looked expectant. Dulcie and Robert studied their steaming soup.

'You've remembered the name of that rose,' guessed Dorothy.

'You've had another wonderful donation for the mission school,' guessed Dimity.

'Better than that,' smiled Charles. 'Our dear friends here are to be married.'

A hubbub of congratulations broke out, and Dimity was beginning to wonder if the soup should be returned to the stove when Robert took charge and said:

'Thank you on behalf of us both. You can guess how much it means to us to meet again here and to give you the news.'

'Do you want to make a speech?' asked Dimity anxiously. 'I can easily reheat the soup.'

'He can make one when we toast them in my best claret during the next course,' Charles told her. 'I suppose we should really have champagne, but we don't have such a thing here.'

'I'm so glad,' said Agnes. 'The only time I had champagne it went straight to my forehead in an icy lump. I had to have a cup of tea to thaw it.'

But Agnes's sole experience of champagne created little interest in the face of this stupendous news of the coming wedding, and the rest of the meal passed in happy conversation about the couple's future plans.

Later, Charles took Robert aside to show him the letter which he had received from Frederick Fennel.

'Oh, this is Miss Fothergill's good work,' he said, studying the immaculate typing.

'Miss Fothergill? His secretary?' guessed Charles.

'Secretary, housekeeper and nurse, all rolled into one,' Robert told him. 'She's looked after him for years. I think he has left her everything in his will, and quite right, too.'

He gave a sudden start, and dropped the letter. His face was pink as he fumbled in his breast pocket and drew out an envelope which he handed to Charles.

'I almost forgot among all our excitement. Frederick asked me to deliver this personally.'

He bent to retrieve the dropped letter from the floor while the rector opened the envelope. There was silence while Charles studied the enclosure.

He looked up at last, and spoke huskily. 'He has sent a donation. An overwhelmingly generous one. For five thousand pounds. I can scarcely believe it. It will be such a relief to Harold. I know he has been grieving about the small sum we have been able to collect here.'

'Wonderful!' said Robert. 'But it doesn't really surprise me. He took such a great interest in hearing about the mission school and our celebrations. Miss Fothergill told me that he was so cheered by all that was happening.'

The rector looked suddenly diffident. 'I hope this won't make any difference to Miss Fothergill's future?'

Robert laughed. 'No difference at all. Frederick Fennel is an exceptionally rich man, and whatever he leaves Miss Fothergill will support her in the greatest comfort for the rest of her life.'

'I am relieved to hear it. Sometimes old people do odd things with their possessions.'

'Not Frederick,' Robert assured him. 'He has more sense in money matters than all the Bank of England directors rolled into one.'

'I am greatly relieved. Miss Fothergill seems an admirable person.'

'Miss Fothergill is worth her weight – and that's considerable, let me say – in gold. And when you come to visit us I will take you and Dimity to see Frederick and Miss Fothergill.'

'We shall look forward to it,' the rector told him. 'I shall write at once to Mr Fennel to thank him for this wonderful gift. I notice you talk of Frederick, and not Mr Fennel, so what is Miss Fothergill's Christian name?'

'I've no idea,' confessed Robert, 'and even if I knew, I should never dare to use it. Miss Fothergill is certainly a saint, but she's a dragon as well.'

Laughing, the two men went to join the others.

*

Later Charles drew Harold into his study and showed him the cheque. He had never seen his friend so moved. Harold's hands trembled as he held the cheque, and he spoke with emotion.

'It's unbelievable! What a relief this is, Charles! I've worried so much about it in these last few weeks, and now this means that we can really send something worthwhile to the mission. God bless Frederick Fennel, and I mean that sincerely.'

There was another shower of rain during the afternoon, and the people of Thrush Green began to look out mackintoshes and umbrellas for the evening's festivities.

'How sensible of Alan Lester to have an indoor event,' remarked Winnie to Jenny, as they sipped their tea by the drawing-room fire.

'And Mr Henstock too,' said Jenny. 'That's one good thing about religious affairs – they're under cover.'

Winnie could not help feeling that this was a somewhat diminishing view of church festivals, but let it pass.

As it grew dark, activity increased on the green. Percy Hodge arrived in his Land Rover with the sack of potatoes. The scoutmaster appeared with his troop who were to cook and distribute Percy's largesse, and Albert Piggott was seen tottering across from his house carrying a paraffin can in case the bonfire was sulky because of the night's downpour.

Luckily, the rain had stopped by the time the celebrations were due to begin, and although the wind was boisterous it was not as savage as it had been during the night.

Charles Henstock drove his party up the hill from Lulling, and met Harold, Isobel, Dorothy and Agnes walking from their house.

A great crowd was gathering, and even the three Miss Love-locks appeared, having been transported by the local taxi.

'Cor!' said Albert to Percy. 'That must have hurt them old ducks, paying out for Bert Nobbs' old banger!'

'Shows how much they wanted to take part,' replied Percy with approval.

It had been agreed that the youngest scout should have the honour of igniting the bonfire. A diminutive figure, brandishing a flaming torch made from a fire-lighter tied to a long dry stick, leapt to his task and, to everyone's relief, the bonfire began to crackle and blaze.

By the light of the flames Nathaniel Patten's statue showed clearly. The children's garland encircled his neck adding a raffish touch to his Victorian garb. Alan Lester thought his pupils had made a very good job of this, their own idea, and felt a pang of pride.

He was there with his wife Margaret and their two daughters, among many other parents now in charge of their own excited offspring.

Suddenly the first rocket went up. It was Harold Shoosmith's suggestion that fireworks should add to the general rejoicing, and certainly there was something wonderfully exhilarating about the bangs and crackles, the whooshing and waving, the sparkle and whirling of innumerable lights, against the blackness of the autumn sky.

There was constant movement, too, among the company as friends met and mingled, the scouts scurried about their cooking duties and the excited children scampered about enjoying the last few hours of this never-to-be-forgotten celebration.

It was ten o'clock before the fire began to die down, and the last Catherine wheel had slowed its whizzing to a stop. The potatoes had been eaten, the scouts congratulated, and the crowd began to straggle away as soon as the final 'Hip, hip, hooray!' had been raised by the rector.

The Lovelock sisters departed early, taken back to their home by Harold. Robert Wilberforce and his betrothed also set off before the last cheers, and there was much speculation about the pair as they walked across the green to their car, Robert's arm protectively around his companion.

Soon only the scoutmaster and his valiant troop remained. It was the scouts' duty to see that the fire was safe to leave, and very zealously they discharged their responsibilities. The fact that an occasional baked potato turned up was an added bonus.

Now that the flames had gone and only a dim glow came from the hot ashes, it was possible to see the stars shining above Thrush Green. The wind had dropped to a light breeze, hardly enough to rustle the leaves of the chestnut trees, or to stir the trailing geraniums in Mr Jones's hanging baskets against the stone walls of The Two Pheasants.

At midnight Harold Shoosmith was alone downstairs. His spirits were buoyant. How wonderfully well everything had turned out, after his worries! Isobel and their two guests had retired an hour earlier, tired by the excitements of the day. Tomorrow Agnes and Dorothy would return to Barton-on-Sea, and the household would be as usual again. Frankly, Harold would be glad of it.

But, as well as relief, Harold realized that there would be a sense of anti-climax after the activity of the last months. The excitement of the search was over. The outcome had been deeply satisfying, but what lay ahead?

He opened the front door and walked down the path to the open stretch of grass where Nathaniel Patten stood beneath the night sky. The air was cool. How often, thought Harold, must Nathaniel have longed for this cool freshness, as he himself had done, under the burning African sky?

These immediate surroundings had changed little since the time when Nathaniel had set out, as a young man, for Bristol, accompanied by his older friend, mentor and benefactor, the good rector of Thrush Green.

How many lives those two had touched! His own, for one. He had chosen to come to Thrush Green on his retirement because he revered the memory of Nathaniel whose work he had admired in Africa.

Here he had met Isobel and made her his wife. Here he had revived the memory of Nathaniel Patten and caused this statue to be raised. Pride in their most famous son had been rekindled in present-day Thrush Green, and the work of his mission in Africa honoured.

It was through Nathaniel's letters that the true greatness of Octavius Fennel, one-time rector of this parish, had been discovered. It was those letters and the rector's own diary which had inspired so many people to carry on the good work begun so long-ago.

And Robert Wilberforce and Dulcie Mulloy would not have met but for Nathaniel Patten. It was a happy thought.

What was more, Nathaniel's mission could continue, thanks to good friends and, in particular, the generous and unseen Frederick Fennel. Celebrations at Thrush Green had been justified.

Harold looked with affection at his old friend. The garland around his bronze neck was fast withering, but his memory would stay fresh with all at Thrush Green.

The words which the congregation had sung that morning came back to Harold.

> *And their work continueth,*
> *Broad and deep continueth*
> *Greater than their knowing.*

Far away and close at hand, thought Harold, that was true.

He returned home, closed the door, and went, greatly content, to bed.

If you have enjoyed *Celebrations at Thrush Green*
here is a taste of Miss Read's acclaimed Fairacre series

Village School

Available in Orion Paperback
ISBN 978-0-7528-7744-0
UK £7.99

1. EARLY MORNING

The first day of term has a flavour that is all its own; a whiff of lazy days behind and a foretaste of the busy future. The essential thing, for a village schoolmistress on such a day, is to get up early.

I told myself this on a fine September morning, ten minutes after switching off the alarm clock. The sun streamed into the bedroom, sparking little rainbows from the mirror's edge; and outside the rooks cawed noisily from the tops of the elm trees in the churchyard. From their high look-out the rooks had a view of the whole village of Fairacre clustered below them; the village which had been my home now for five years.

I had enjoyed those five years – the children, the little school, the pleasure of running my own school-house and of taking a part in village life. True, at first, I had had to walk as warily as Agag; many a slip of the tongue caused me, even now, to go hot and cold at the mere memory, but at last, I believed, I was accepted, if not as a proper native, at least as 'Miss Read up the School,' and not as 'that new woman pushing herself forward!'

I wondered if the rooks, whose clamour was increasing with the warmth of the sun, could see as far as Tyler's Row at the end of the village. Here lived Jimmy Waites and Joseph Coggs, two little boys who were to enter school today. Another new child was also coming, and this thought prodded me finally out of bed and down the narrow stairs.

I filled the kettle from the pump at the sink and switched it on. The new school year had begun.

Tyler's Row consists of four thatched cottages and very pretty they look. Visitors always exclaim when they see them, sighing ecstatically and saying how much they would like to live there. As a realist I am always constrained to point out the disadvantages that lurk behind the honeysuckle.

The thatch is in a bad way, and though no rain has yet dripped through into the dark bedrooms below, it most certainly will before long. There is no doubt about a rat or two running along the ridge, as spry as you please, reconnoitring probably for a future home; and the starlings and sparrows find it a perfect resting-place.

'They ought to do something for us,' Mrs Waites told me, but as 'They,' meaning the landlord, is an old soldier living with his sister in the next village on a small pension and the three shillings he gets a week from each cottage (when he is lucky), it is hardly surprising that the roof is as it is.

There is no drainage of any sort and no damp-course. The brick floors sweat and clothes left hanging near a wall produce a splendid crop of prussian blue mildew in no time.

Washing-up water, soap-suds and so on are either emptied into a deep hole by the hedge or flung broadcast over the garden.

The plants flourish on this treatment, particularly the rows of Madonna lilies which are the envy of the village. The night-cart, now a tanker-lorry, elects to call in the heat of the day, usually between twelve and one o'clock, once a week. The sewerage is carried through the only living-room and out into the road, for the edification of the school-children who are making their way home to dinner, most probably after a hygiene lesson on the importance of cleanliness.

In the second cottage Jimmy Waites was being washed. He stood on a chair by the shallow stone sink, submitting meekly to his mother's ministrations. She had twisted the corner of the face-flannel into a formidable radish and was turning it remorselessly round and round inside his left ear. He wore new corduroy trousers, dazzling braces and a woollen vest. Hanging on a line which was slung across the front of the mantelpiece, was a bright blue-and-red-checked shirt, American style. His mother intended that her Jimmy should do her credit on his first day at school.

She was a blonde, lively woman married to a farm-worker as fair as herself. 'I always had plenty of spirit,' she said once, 'Why, even during the war when I was alone I kept cheerful!' She did, too, from all accounts told by her more puritanical neighbours; and certainly none of us is so silly as to ask questions about Cathy, the only dark child of the six, born during her husband's absence in 1944.

Cathy, while her brother was being scrubbed, was feeding the hens at the end of the garden. She threw out handfuls of mixed wheat and oats which she had helped to glean nearly a year ago. This was a treat for the chickens and they squawked and screeched as they fought for their breakfast.

Their noise brought one of the children who lived next door to a gap in the hedge that divided the gardens. Joseph was about five, of gipsy stock, with eyes as dark and pathetic as a monkey's. Cathy had promised to take him with her and Jimmy on this his first school morning. This was a great concession on the part of Mrs Waites as the raggle-taggle family next door was normally ignored.

'Don't you play with them dirty kids,' she warned her own children, 'or you'll get Nurse coming down the school to look at you special!' And this dark threat was enough.

3

But today Cathy looked at Joseph with a critical eye and spoke first.

'You ready?'

The child nodded in reply.

'You don't look like it,' responded his guardian roundly. 'You wants to wash the jam off of your mouth. Got a hanky?'

'No,' said Joe, bewildered.

'Well, you best get one. Bit of rag'll do, but Miss Read lets off awful if you forgets your hanky. Where's your mum?'

'Feeding baby.'

'Tell her about the rag,' ordered Cathy, 'and buck up. Me and Jim's nearly ready.' And swinging the empty tin dipper she skipped back into her house.

Meanwhile, the third new child was being prepared. Linda was eight years old, fat and phlegmatic, and the pride of her fond mother's heart. She was busy buttoning her new red shoes while her mother packed a piece of chocolate for her elevenses at playtime.

The Moffats had only lived in Fairacre for three weeks, but we had watched their bungalow being built for the last six months.

'Bathroom and everything!' I had been told, 'and one of those hatchers to put the dishes through to save your legs. Real lovely!'

The eagle eye of the village was upon the owners whenever they came over from Caxley, our nearest market town, to see the progress of their house. Mrs Moffat had been seen measuring the windows for curtains and holding patterns of material against the distempered walls.

'Thinks herself someone, you know!' I was told later. 'Never so much as spoke to me in the road!'

'Perhaps she was shy.'

'Humph!'

'Or deaf, even.'

'None so deaf as those that won't hear,' was the tart rejoin-der. Mrs Moffat, alas! was already suspected of that heinous village crime known as 'putting on side.'

One evening, during the holidays, she had brought the child to see me. I was gardening and they both looked askance at my bare legs and dirty hands. It was obvious that she tended to cosset her rather smug daughter and that appearances meant a lot to her, but I liked her and guessed that the child was intelligent and would work well. That her finery would also excite adverse comment among the other children I also sur-mised. Mrs Moffat's aloofness was really only part of her town upbringing, and once she realized the necessity for exchanging greetings with every living soul in the village, no matter how pressing or distracting one's own business, she would soon be accepted by the other women.

Linda would come into my class. She would be in the young-est group, among those just sent up from the infants' room where they had spent three years under Miss Clare's benign rule. Joseph and Jimmy would naturally go straight into her charge.

At twenty to nine I hung up the tea towel, closed the back door of the school-house and stepped across the playground to the school.

Above me the rooks still chattered. Far below they could see, converging upon the school lane, little knots of children from all quarters of the village. Cathy had Jimmy firmly by the hand: Joseph's grimy paw she disdained to hold, and he trailed behind her, his dark eyes apprehensive.

Linda Moffat, immaculate in starched pink gingham, walked

primly beside her mother; while behind and before, running, dawdling, shouting or whistling, ran her future school fellows.

Through the sunny air another sound challenged the rooks' chorus. The school bell began to ring out its morning greeting.

2. OUR SCHOOL

The school at Fairacre was built in 1880, and as it is a church school it is strongly ecclesiastical in appearance. The walls are made of local stone, a warm grey in colour, reflecting summer light with honeyed mellowness, but appearing dull and dejected when the weather is wet. The roof is high and steeply-pitched and the stubby bell-tower thrusts its little Gothic nose skywards, emulating the soaring spire of St Patrick's, the parish church, which stands next door.

The windows are high and narrow, with pointed tops. Children were not encouraged, in those days, to spend their working time in gazing out at the world, and, sitting stiffly in the well of the room, wearing sailor suits or stout zephyr and serge frocks, their only view was of the sky, the elm trees and St Patrick's spire. Today their grandchildren and great-grandchildren have exactly the same view; just this lofty glimpse of surrounding loveliness.

The building consists of two rooms divided by a partition of glass and wood. One room houses the infants, aged five, six and seven years of age, under Miss Clare's benevolent eye. The other room is my classroom where the older children of junior age stay until they are eleven when they pass on to a secondary school, either at Caxley, six miles away, or in the neighbouring village of Beech Green, where the children stay until they are fifteen.

A long lobby runs behind these two rooms, the length of the building; it is furnished with pegs for coats, a low stone sink for the children to wash in, and a high new one for washing-up the dinner things. An electric copper is a recent acquisition, and very handsome it is; but although we have electricity installed here there is no water laid on to the school.

This is, of course, an appalling problem, for there is no water to drink – and children get horribly thirsty – no water for washing hands, faces, cleansing cuts and grazes, for painting, for mixing paste or watering plants or filling flower vases; and, of course, no water for lavatories.

We overcome this problem in two ways. A large galvanized iron tank on wheels is filled with rainwater collected from the roof, and this, when we have skimmed off the leaves and twigs and rescued the occasional frog, serves most of our needs. The electric copper is filled in the morning from this source and switched on after morning playtime to be ready for washing not only the crockery and cutlery after dinner but also the stone floor of the lobby.

I bring two buckets of drinking water across the playground from the school-house where there is an excellent well, but we must do our own heating, so that a venerable black kettle stands on my stove throughout the winter months, purring in a pleasantly domestic fashion, ready for emergencies. The electric kettle, in my own kitchen, serves us at other times.

The building is solid structurally and kept in repair by the church authorities whose property it is. One defect, however, it seems impossible to overcome. A skylight, strategically placed over the headmistress's desk, lets in not only light, but rain. Generations of local builders have clambered over the roof and sworn and sawn and patched and pulled at our skylight – but in vain. The gods have willed otherwise, and year after year Pluvius drops his pennies into a bucket placed below for the purpose, the clanging muffled by a dishcloth folded to fit the bottom.

The school stands at right angles to the road and faces across the churchyard to the church. A low dry-stone wall runs along by the road dividing it from the churchyard, school playground and the school-house garden. Behind this the country slopes away, falling slightly at first, then rising, in swelling folds, up into the full majesty of the downs which sweep across these southern counties for mile upon mile. The air is always bracing, and in the winter the wind is a bitter foe, and that quality of pure light, which is peculiar to downland country, is here very noticeable.

The children are hardy and though, quite naturally, they take their surroundings for granted, I think that they are aware of the fine views around them. The girls particularly are fond of flowers, birds, insects and all the minutiae of natural life, guarding jealously any rare plant against outsiders' prying eyes, and having a real knowledge of the whereabouts and uses of many plants and herbs.

The boys like to dismiss such things as 'girls' stuff,' but they too can find the first mushrooms, sloes or blackberries for their mothers or for me; and most of the birds' nests are known as soon as they are built. Luckily, stealing eggs and rifling nests seem to be on the wane, though occasional culprits are brought to stern judgment at my desk. They suffer, I think, more from the tongues of the girls in the playground in matters like this, for there is no doubt about it that the girls are more sympathetic to living things and pour scorn and contumely on any young male tyrants.

In one corner of the small, square playground is the inevitable pile of coke for the two slow combustion stoves. These coke piles seem to be a natural feature of all country schools. This is considered by the children, a valuable adjunct to playtime activities. A favourite game is to run scrunchily up the pile and then to slither down in gritty exhilaration. Throwing it at each other, or at a noisy object such as the rainwater tank, is also much enjoyed, hands being wiped perfunctorily down the fronts of jackets or on the seats of trousers before the beginning of writing lessons. All these joys are strictly forbidden, of course, which adds to the fearful delight.

Furthest from the wall by the road at the other side of the playground grows a clump of elm trees, and their gnarled roots, which add to the hazards of the playground's surface, are a favourite place to play.

The recesses are rooms, larders, cupboards or gardens, and the ivy leaves from the wall are used for plates and provisions, and twigs for knives and forks. Sometimes they play shops among the roots, paying each other leaves and bearing away conkers, acorns and handfuls of gravel as their purchases. I like to hear the change in their voices as they become shopkeepers or customers. They affect a high dictatorial tone of voice when they assume adult status, quite unlike the warm burr of their everyday conversations.

The fields lie two or three feet below the level of the playground and a scrubby hedge of hazel and hawthorn marks this boundary. The sloping bank down is scored by dozens of little bare paths, worn by generations of sturdy boots and corduroy breeches.

Altogether our playground is a good one – full of possibilities for resourceful children and big enough to allow shopkeepers, mothers and fathers, cowboys and spacemen to carry on their urgent affairs very happily together.

On this first morning of term Miss Clare had already arrived when I walked over at a quarter to nine. Her bicycle, as upright and as ancient as its owner, was propped just inside the lobby door.

The school had that indefinable first-morning smell compounded of yellow soap, scrubbed floorboards and black-lead. The tortoise stove gleamed like an ebony monster; even the vent-pipe which soared aloft towards the pitch-pine roof was blackened as far as Mrs Pringle, the school cleaner, could reach. Clean newspaper covered the freshly-hearthstoned surroundings of the stove – which officially remained unlit until October – and the guard, just as glossy, was neatly placed round the edges of the outspread *News of the World*.

My desk had that bare tidy look that it only wears for an hour or so on this particular morning of term; and the inkstand, an imposing affair of mahogany and brass, shone in splendour. I wondered as I walked through to Miss Clare's room just how quickly its shelf would remain unencumbered by the chalk, beads, raincoat buttons, paper clips, raffia needles and drawing pins that were its normal burden.

Miss Clare was taking a coat-hanger out of her big canvas hold-all. She is very careful of her clothes, and is grieved to see the casual way in which the children sling their coats, haphazard, on to the pegs in the lobby. Her own coat is always smoothed methodically over its hanger and hung on the back of the classroom door. The children watch, fascinated, when she removes her gloves, for she blows into them several times before folding them neatly together. Her sensible felt hat has a shelf to itself inside the needlework cupboard.

Miss Clare has taught here for nearly forty years, with only one break, when she nursed her mother through her last illness twelve years ago. She started here as a monitress at the age of thirteen, and was known officially, until recently, as 'A Supplementary Uncertificated Teacher.' Her knowledge of local family history is far-reaching and of inestimable value to the teaching of our present pupils. I like to hear the older people talk of her. 'Always a stickler for tidiness,' the butcher told me, 'the only time I was smacked in the babies' class was when Miss Clare found me kicking another boy's cap round the floor.'

Miss Clare is of commanding appearance, tall and thin, with beautiful white hair, which is kept in place with an invisible hair-net. Even on the wildest day, when the wind shrieks across the downs, Miss Clare walks round the playground looking immaculate. She is now over sixty, and her teaching methods have of late been looked upon by some visiting inspectors with a slightly pitying eye. They are, they say, too formal; the children should have more activity, and the classroom is unnaturally quiet for children of that age. This may be, but for all that, or perhaps because of that, Miss Clare is a very valuable teacher, for in the first place the children are happy, they are fond of Miss Clare, and she creates for them an atmosphere of serenity and quiet which means that they can work well and cheerfully, really laying the foundations of elementary knowledge on which I can build so much more quickly when they come up into my class.

Her home is two miles away, on the outskirts of the next village of Beech Green. She has lived there ever since she was six, a solemn little girl in high-buttoned boots and ringlets, in the cottage which her father thatched himself. He was a thatcher by trade, and many of the cottages in the surrounding villages are decorated with the ornate criss-crossing and plaiting which he loved to do. He was much in demand at harvest time for thatching ricks, and Miss Clare often makes 'rick-dollies' of straw for the children like the ones her father used to put on top of the newly-thatched stacks.

In the corner of the room John Burton was pulling lustily at the bell-rope. He stopped as I came in.

'Five minutes' rest,' I said, 'then another pull or two to tell the others that it's time to get into lines in the playground.'

Miss Clare and I exchanged holiday news while she unlocked her desk and took out her new register, carefully shrouded in fresh brown paper. She had covered mine for me too, at the end of last term, and written in the names of our new classes in her sloping copper-plate hand.

We should have forty children altogether this term; eighteen in the infants' room and twenty-two in mine; and though our numbers might seem small, compared with the monstrous regiments of forty and fifty to a class in town schools, the age range, of course, would be a considerable handicap.

I should have five children in my lowest group who would be nearly eight years old and these would still have difficulty in reading fluently and with complete understanding. At the other

end of the classroom would be my top group, consisting of
three children, including Cathy Waites, who would be taking
the examination which would decide their future schooling at
eleven. These children would need particular care in being
shown how to tackle arithmetical problems, how to understand
written questions and, more important still, how to set out their
answers and express themselves generally, in clear and straight-
forward language.

Miss Clare's youngest group would consist of the two new
little boys, Jimmy Waites and Joseph Coggs, as well as the
twins, Diana and Helen, who had entered late last term owing
to measles and had learnt very little. Miss Clare was of the
opinion, knowing something of their family history, that they
might well be in her bottom group for years.

'What can you expect,' she said, looking at the hieroglyphics
that passed for writing on their blackboards, 'their grandfather
never stuck at one job for more than a week and the boy took
after him. Added to that he married a girl with as much sense as
himself, and these two are the result.'

'I'll get the doctor to look at them specially, when she comes,'
I comforted her, 'I think if they had their adenoids removed
they might be much brighter.'

Miss Clare's snort showed what good she thought this
would do two of the biggest duffers who had ever come into
her hands.

Her aim with the top group in her class will be, first, to see
that they can read, and also write legibly, know their multiplication tables up to six times at least, and be able to do the
four rules of addition, subtraction, multiplication and division,
working with tens and units and shillings and pence. They
should also have a working knowledge of the simple forms of
money, weight and length, and be able to tell the time.

John, who had had his gaze fixed on the ancient wall-clock,

now gave six gigantic tugs on the rope, for it said five minutes to nine, and then, leaping up on to the corner desk, looped it up, out of temptation's way, on to a hook high on the wall.

Outside, we could hear the scuffle of feet and cries of excited children. Together Miss Clare and I walked out into the sunshine to meet our classes.

EARLY DAYS
A Childhood Memoir

* * *

Miss Read

From the author of the bestselling
FAIRACRE and THRUSH GREEN series

'The larks were in joyous frenzy above. The sky was blue, the
now distant wood misty with early buds, and the air was
heady to a London child. A great surge of happiness engulfed
me. This is where I was going to live. I should learn all about
birds and trees and flowers. This is where I belonged . . . This
was the country, and I was at home there.'

Early Days is alive with vibrant childhood memories of an
extended family of grandmas, uncles, aunts and cousins, and
their houses – full of mystery and adventure – where Miss
Read lived in the shadow of the First World War.

At the age of seven, Miss Read moved to a small village in
Kent, into a magical new world where her love of the English
countryside grew – a passion that would be found in her
much-loved novels. Her evocative descriptions of the village
school, the joys of exploring the woods and lanes, toffee-
making and riding on the corn-chandler's cart, vividly convey
this time as one of the happiest of her life.

Full of unforgettable characters, tender memories and the
colourful intrigues of everyday life, *Early Days* is a charming
and affectionate insight into the childhood of a bestselling
author, and a bygone era.

ISBN: 978 0 7528 8220 8
UK £7.99